## THEY'RE GOING TO DESTROY CALIFORNIA ...

*Dr. Harold W. Smith, head of CURE, toyed with a letter opener as he listened to Remo.*

*"All right," he said. "I understand. Do you have any leads? Anything at all?"*

*"Nothing. I think Dr. Quake's machine is involved. But what about the million?"*

*"Stay where you are," Smith said. "I'll call you back."*

*Blackmailing the government. It was unthinkable.*

*But duty required that he report the message to the President. It was a decision for the Chief Executive to make.*

*In Washington, the president picked up the secret telephone and listened as Smith explained the circumstances.*

*The President reacted immediately.*

*"My decision is this. We will pay them the million dollars."*

*"As you wish," Smith said. He hung up the telephone and dialed Remo Williams' number. The president was wrong. He should not pay.*

### IT WAS A JOB FOR THE DESTROYER ...

# THE DESTROYER:
# DR. QUAKE

*by*
*Richard Sapir and Warren Murphy*

PINNACLE BOOKS • NEW YORK CITY

THE DESTROYER: DR. QUAKE

An original Pinnacle Books edition, published for the
first time anywhere.

ISBN: 0-523-00365-X

First printing, September 1972
Second printing, October 1972
Third printing, March 1973
Fourth printing, March 1974

Printed in the United States of America

PINNACLE BOOKS, INC.
275 Madison Avenue
New York, N.Y. 10016

# THE DESTROYER:
# DR. QUAKE

# CHAPTER ONE

Every man owes God a life. California owes Him a disaster, payable about twice a century.

For those people not hurled hundreds of feet in shifting earth; for those not buried alive in their homes along with the fear-triggered refuse of their bodies; for those not deposited deeper than any gravedigger's plan, these disasters are considered a simple geological adjustment. A releasing of pressure.

They are the result of an earth wound called the San Andreas fault, one of the many faults in California which make it a geological time bomb with a mutitude of fuses. All of them burning.

The San Andreas fault runs six hundred miles from Baja California in the South to Mendocino in the North. It is created by the Pacific Plate on the earth's surface going northwest and the North American Continental Plate going southeast at a speed of several inches of year. The seam between those two plates runs the length of California, and when the two plates bump . . . earthquake.

In one small area, east of Los Angeles, in San Aquino County, the plates lock together every so often, building up pressure. When they unlock, about twice every hundred years, nature pays its bi-centennial dues as the plates unleash their tension. For human beings within a few hundred miles, as the earth along the fault lurches, the universe appears to be ending.

For some of them it does.

Many geologists believe the next unspringing of the lock will make any nuclear weapons so far devised look like spears and stones. California is due for a bloodletting unrivalled in recorded history, so say these geologists. It will be in five minutes or in thirty years, but it will be. The earth only waits ... with the human sacrifices enjoying the California sun until their moment in the pit ... a moment in time known only to God.

It was therefore considered unbelievable when official Washington was approached by a man with a plan to harness this terror. And later, it was considered unthinkable that anyone would purposely trigger this disaster.

Unthinkable, until a government geologist in Washington, D.C. heard a detailed account of something he could not believe.

"But that's impossible," he said. "That's as impossible as ... impossible as...."

"Impossible as throwing people into ovens," said the harried visitor from San Aquino County, California.

# CHAPTER TWO

It was impossible. But it was happening right on time.

Birds took flight. Rabbits scurried crazily across the vine-covered fields. Three squirrels scrambled up the dirt road, ignoring cover. Trees swayed, showering leaves like green confetti. Thin red dust rose from the San Aquino countryside as if someone were dynamiting the bowels of California.

Four leading citizens of San Aquino and the county sheriff looked at their watches and groaned, almost in unison. They stood beside a well-polished Lincoln limousine at the entrance of the Gromucci farm where Sheriff Wade Wyatt assured them they could probably see best what would happen, while not being seen looking for it.

"We don't want to let 'em know we're scared, you know," he had told them.

So now the sun was hot, the dust-clogged air made breathing difficult and it had happened.

"I don't believe it," said Harris Feinstein, owner of Feinstein's Department Store. "I see it, but I don't believe it. Does your watch read 3:55 P.M., Les?"

"Yes," said Lester Curpwell IV, president of the First Aquino Trust and Development Company. "Three fifty five. Right on time to the second." Curpwell was in his mid-fifties, taller than Feinstein

9

by an inch and a half, his face strong and smooth, able to show concern but not worry, a face that planned but never schemed. He wore a dark pin-striped suit with white shirt and Princeton tie.

Feinstein was more Hollywood, deeply tanned, his face evidencing meditation and tenderness. He wore a blue blazer and white slacks. Curpwell's shoes were polished black cordovan, Feinstein's soft Italian leather.

"They can do it then," said Feinstein.

"Well, we know they can do this much at least," said Curpwell.

"If they can do this, they can do more," said Feinstein.

"That's right," butted in Sheriff Wade Wyatt. "They said they can do anything. Make any kind of earthquake they want. A little ripple like this. Or boom. The whole works." He waved with his hands, indicating a massive explosion.

"I just don't want to believe it," Feinstein said.

"It looks like a barrage, like after a barrage," said Dourn Rucker, president of Rucker Manufacturing Company. "You know, the dust and everything. Like after a barrage."

"All right. There are good points. We should think about the positive points," said Sonny Boydenhousen, president of Boydenhousen Realty and president of the San Aquino Chamber of Commerce. He was, like Rucker, over six feet tall. Both had pleasant bland faces and bellies going slightly potward. When they wore identical clothes, some people mistook them for twins. Today, they wore gray suits with pink shirts.

"There may be good points," he insisted. "Look, they've showed us they can make an earthquake. But they say they can prevent them. Now if they can,

10

that's great. It'll do wonders for real estate values here. Do you think they're reliable, Wade?"

"I don't know," said Sheriff Wyatt. "All I know's that they did what they said they was going to."

Wyatt was a red-faced balloon of a man with a neat Stetson and a diamond and ruby chip American flag pin in his collar. He wore a .44 with five notches in the grip. He had put the five notches in himself with his own hand, carving very carefully. He said they represented five men. What they represented was a cut finger.

"Eight thousand dollars a month is not a bad price. I say eight thousand dollars a month is reasonable," said Boydenhousen.

"Like after a barrage," said Rucker, still gazing at the dusty field. "Like after a barrage."

"Impossible," said Feinstein.

"Two thousand dollars too much for you?" asked Wyatt, a hint of contempt in his voice. He avoided Curpwell's angry glare. He did not want another lecture on anti-semitism.

"It's not the money. I'd give ten times that for education. I've given more than fifty times that to the hospital. But this is blackmail money. Extortion money. Do you believe that? Do you know what country this is, Wade?"

"Amurrica, Mr. Feinstein, in God blessed America." His chest rose when he said that and he hoisted up his gunbelt lest the sudden loss of belly let it slip to the ground. He had always had trouble with Feinstein, whose bleeding heart seemed always to bleed for the troublemakers, the riffraff, the loafers. Not for businessmen or sheriffs or the good people who made San Aquino one of the nicest little counties in the world.

They had been told they could keep it that way, too, if everyone kept his head and was reasonable.

11

After all, it was a very reasonable proposition. Sheriff Wyatt had been contacted by people over the telephone. They told him they could make earthquakes. As he related it, Sheriff Wyatt had told them to go to hell.

They told him there would be an earthquake the next day at noon. And there was. The smallest possible. Just a tremor. Then they called again. This time, they said, they would give San Aquino another little gift. This time, a number two on the Mercalli intensity scale which measures earthquakes. Birds and small animals would be affected by it and you could feel it in your feet if you stood in an open field. It would happen at 3:55 p.m.

They told Wyatt that they could also deliver the kind of earthquake that buried cities and made civilizations disappear. But they weren't unreasonable. They could also guarantee no earthquakes. And all it would cost was $8,000 a month—$2,000 each from the county's four leading citizens. All very reasonable.

It was just after 3:55 p.m. and they had proved they could do it. But some people were unreasonable.

"Blackmail," Feinstein said again. "You're right, Wade. This is America, and Americans don't pay blackmail."

"I understand how you feel, Harris," Curpwell interrupted. "So do Sonny and Dourn. And I think, if you simplified it a bit, so would the sheriff. But on the other hand, you could think of it not as blackmail, but as insurance. What do you think the people of San Francisco would have paid not to have had 1906?" He did not give Feinstein a chance to answer. "At any rate, think about it. And we'll all meet tonight in my office at 8 o'clock. Then we'll decide."

They drove back to town, mostly in silence, ignoring Wyatt's attempts at conversation as he drove the black limousine.

Feinstein was the last to arrive that night at the private office of Lester Curpwell. The faces all turned to him as he entered the rich panelled office and locked the door behind him.

He took an envelope from his back pocket, dropped it on the table. It contained $2,000 in fives, tens and twenties, none of them new.

"That's it," he said. "Two thousand. My one and only contribution to this extortion racket. We can buy a month. I'm going to Washington tonight to tell the government."

"Do you remember we were warned?," Rucker said. "If we talk, there'll be an earthquake. A giant one. Everyone in San Aquino may die."

"I don't think so," Feinstein said. "They'll have their eight thousand. And no one has to know that I've gone to Washington."

"You don't think so?" said Boydenhousen loudly. "You don't think so? Well, I can't live by what you think.

"Look," he said. "We opened up this community to you Feinsteins, way back in the 1920's when a lot of towns just weren't too all-fired happy to have your kind. We welcomed you. And I'm not saying you didn't like build the hospital and everything, but I am saying, you're a part of this community, dammit, and you don't have any right to endanger us. That's what I'm saying."

"And I'm saying, Sonny Boydenhousen, that we weren't all that welcome, but we made some good friends, of which there was never a Boydenhousen, which also is no great loss. What I'm saying is I'm part of a larger community and that's every poor town in this state. Every town that may someday be

13

digging its babies out of piles of rock because they can't afford to pay. That's what I'm thinking."

"And I'm thinking," yelled Sonny Boydenhousen, "how fucking grateful I am that we can feel safe and not have to worry about that. How grateful that my kids are safe from that. You want to kill my kids, Harris? Is that it?"

Harris Feinstein lowered his gaze to the corporate table, a glistening, polished oak masterpiece, handed down from Curpwell to Curpwell, through generations of San Aquino patricians. The Curpwells were good people. He knew their family well. So did his father.

That was one of the grievously hard things about this decision. He wavered for a minute, looking at the faces of the men around him. Friend, enemy, he did not want to endanger one life. There were part of his life, all of them. They meant, really meant, more to him than someone living in Los Angeles or San Francisco or any of the other California communities that might be the next to be blackmailed for earthquake insurance.

Really, Harris, he told himself, aren't you being a bit prideful? Remember how you and Sonny were keychain guards on the 1938 San Aquino football team, the year you beat Los Angeles Gothic. And how when you were labelled the dirtiest football player in the state, the whole team celebrated by stealing a keg of beer and getting drunk? And Wyatt. Wyatt never made the football team, saying he had to hunt to keep food on the family table. But everyone knew the reason Wade Wyatt went hunting in the fall was because he didn't want to be accused of chickening out on football. Wade's father always put food on the table, but Wade had seen a movie in

14

which the young frontiersman didn't go to school because he had to hunt for the family's supper.

And Dourn, loverboy Dourn. Dourn who got Pearl Fansworth pregnant in the junior year of high school and how Pearl had to go away. And how Dourn got Sonny's sister pregnant in his senior year and how he had to marry her.

And of course, Les Curpwell. A beautiful human being.

Harris Feinstein lowered his eyes to the table again and wondered why everything wasn't as clear as when he was in school or studying the Talmud with his father. Then, things were clear. Now, nothing was clear but that he felt very unintelligent and longed for someone to tell him what was right and good and which way to go. But that could not be. God had given him a mind. And meant for him to use it. So Harris Feinstein looked at his friends, and at the jeweled flag pin on Sheriff Wade Wyatt's collar, and he said, very sadly and very slowly:

"I must do what I must do and it is not an easy thing. And I am only sorry that you are not doing this thing with me."

His envelope sat on the table. Sonny Boydenhousen took a similar envelope from his attache case and put it on the table. Curpwell added another and so did Dourn Rucker.

Sheriff Wyatt gathered the envelopes together and pushed them into a small plastic garbage bag. The four other men watched silently as he closed the bag with a red covered wire tie. He made a small bow of it.

"Leakproof," he said. No one smiled. Harris Feinstein avoided the other men's eyes.

"Well, goodbye," he said.

"You going to Washington?" asked Dourn Rucker.

"Tonight," said Harris Feinstein.

"Oh," said Sonny Boydenhousen. "Look. Those things I said about your family being welcomed here in San Aquino, like we were doing you a favor ... well, you know what I mean."

"I know," said Feinstein.

"I guess you're going to do it," said Curpwell.

"Yes."

"I wish I could say I thought you're doing the right thing," said Boydenhousen. "And I wish I could say I would want to do it with you. But I think you're doing a very wrong thing."

"Maybe, but. . . ." Harris Feinstein did not finish his sentence. When he had shut the large brass-studded door to the most hallowed sanctum of power in San Aquino, the Curpwell office, Sheriff Wyatt made a suggestion.

He did so fingering the notches on his gun.

Les Curpwell didn't bother to answer and Dourn Rucker told Sheriff Wyatt that Feinstein would probably pound him into dentifrice anyway, so Wyatt might as well put away the gun.

Curpwell noted that Feinstein might be right. So did Rucker. So did Boydenhousen. But they all agreed that they all had families, and hell, weren't they all really doing enough—paying for everyone who lived in the town and county of San Aquino?

"I mean we're acting like damned philanthropists. Two thousand dollars from each of us, every god-damned month. We didn't ask anyone else to chip in, not even the sheriff because he doesn't have the money," said Rucker. "So shit, nobody's got any right to point a finger at us. Nobody."

"All I know," said Boydenhousen, "is that we've got a chance to be quakeproof. Now going to Washington may louse it up. And that's just not right. We should just pay up and keep quiet."

"Gentlemen, you are right and Harris is wrong," said Les Curpwell. "Only I'm just not sure how much righter we are."

Then Sheriff Wyatt announced a plan.

"Look, I get my instructions on delivery in the morning. Suppose I go to the place, wherever it is, and hide. You know, camouflage, like the Ranger training I picked up in National Guard summer camp. Then, when whoever it is comes for the money, I follow. All right. When I get 'em all, using my Ranger techniques, bam! I let them have it. Let loose with a Carbine. Bam. Hand grenades. Whoosh! Bam! Whoosh! Kill or be killed. I give you the word of a captain in the National Guard of the State of California."

The voting of the three leaders of San Aquino was unanimous.

"Just leave the money where they tell you."

• • •

Les Curpwell sat in his office a long time after all the others had left. Then he walked to his desk and telephoned a close friend who was an aide to the President.

"If what you say is true, Les, they have the power to gut the whole state of California."

"I think it's true," Curpwell said.

"Wow. All I can say is *Wow*. I'm going right to the top with this. I can get to see the President immediately on this one."

The aide was shocked by the President's reaction. He had delivered the report thoroughly and professionally, the way Les Curpwell had given it to him.

Lester Curpwell IV, former OSS agent, thoroughly-reliable Lester Curpwell. The time. The threats. The earthquake. No guesses. Hard information.

But when the aide was through, the President said:

"Okay. Forget about it. Tell no one."

"But, sir. Don't you believe me?"

"I believe you."

"But this is something for the FBI. I can give them all the details."

"You will give nothing to anyone. You will be absolutely quiet about this. Absolutely. That is all. Good evening."

The aide rose to leave but the President halted him.

"Leave your notes here, please. And don't worry. We're not defenseless."

"Yes sir," said the aide, placing his notes on the President's desk.

When the aide had gone, the President threw the notes into an electric wastebasket by his desk, the basket that assured that no information would leave with the garbage. It ground up the notes with a whir.

Then the President left his office and went to his bedroom. From the top bureau drawer, he removed a red telephone and lifted the receiver.

Before one ring completed itself, the call was answered.

"We're on it," came the voice.

"The California thing?"

"Yes."

"That was fast," the President said.

"It has to be," the voice answered.

"These people, whoever they are, could trigger a disaster," the President said.

"Yes, they could."

"Are you going to use that special person?"

"Is there anything else, Mr. President?"

"Well, I wanted to know if you're going to use him?"

"It wouldn't do you any good, sir, to know. You might be tempted to look for his picture in crowds if the newspapers should have something to photograph out there."

"Suppose you use that person and lose him?" the President asked.

"Then we lose him."

"I see."

"If it would make you feel any better, sir, I think we have a good line on this thing. The perpetrators are dead meat."

"Then you will use him?"

"Good night, Mr. President."

The phone clicked and the President returned the telephone to the bureau drawer. As he covered the phone with one of his shirts, he wondered what that special person's name was.

# CHAPTER THREE

His name was Remo and he had not read more than one of the geology books shipped to him at the hotel in St. Thomas. He had not looked at the scale models of California's crust for more than five minutes, and he had paid no attention at all to the tutor who had thought he was explaining faults and earthquakes to a salesman newly hired by a geological instruments' company.

Not that Remo hadn't tried. He read the basic college geology book, the primer, from cover to cover. When he was finished, his memory floated with cartoons of rocks, water and very stiff people. He understood everything he had read; he just didn't care about it. He forgot 85 per cent of the book the day after he read it, and 14 per cent more the day after that.

What he remembered was the modified Mercalli intensity scale. He did not remember what it was, just that there was a thing geologists called the modified Mercalli intensity scale.

He wondered about it as he stood on the cliff overlooking an outcropping of green moss-covered rocks. Maybe he was standing on a modified Mercalli intensity scale. Well, whether he was or not, the little grass air strip that began about one hundred yards farther on along the edge of the cliff and cut into the flatness of the cliff top was where at least five men would die. They would be killed very well and very quietly; in the end no one would think it anything but an accident.

Killing, Remo knew very well.

He lounged against a gracefully curving tree, feeling the fresh salt air of the Caribbean warm his body as it massaged his soul. The sun burned his strong face. He closed his deep-set eyes, folded his arms over his striped polo shirt. He lifted one leg to rest beneath his buttocks on the tree trunk. He could hear the voices of the three men sitting near their little farm truck. *They were sure, mon, that no white fellow could sneak through the jungle near them. Certain, mon. They were also sure, mon, that the delivery was soon. If there was any trouble, however, they had their carbines and could put a hole in a mon at two hundred yards and do it right propah. Yessirree. Right propah.* Through his bloody genitals, eh, Rufus?

Remo turned his head to get sun on the right side of his neck. His face was healing and he had been promised that this was the last time it would be changed. He looked now almost as he had looked when he had been a living, recorded, human being with fingerprints in Washington, a credit card, bills and an identity as Remo Williams, policeman. He liked that face. It was the most human face he had ever had. His.

And even if someone who had known him by sight should see him and think the face was familiar, they would be sure it was not Patrolman Remo Williams. Because Patrolman Remo Williams had died in New Jersey's electric chair years ago for killing a drug pusher in an alley.

The pusher was dead all right, but in point of fact, Remo Williams hadn't shot him. So, in the spirit of justice, Remo Williams didn't die in the electric chair either. But the whole charade was a convenient government way to remove his fingerprints from all files and his identity from all files—to create the man who didn't exist.

The Caribbean felt good to be near, like a life force. Remo languished on the precipice of sleep. One of the men near the truck, Rufus, told the others he was afraid.

"And if anything goes wrong, mon, I'm going to kill those white boys. This is the big stuff we're dealing with. I'll shoot those coppers too, I will. Yessir, mon. One dead copper what deals with Old Rufus."

Well, Rufus, if you want to shoot white men, feel free. It might even give me more sleep, thought Remo. He listened for a far-off engine and thought he deciphered it out of the gentle lapping of the waves below.

Rufus also had advice. He told his two companions not to worry.

"Worry about what, Rufus?"

"Just don't worry about what the old lady on the hill says."

"I did not know she said something, mon." The voices were the sing-song clipped British of the Caribbean, the remnant of a not altogether good colonialism which was not altogether bad, either. The Caribbean seemed to be divorced from normal morality.

"About today and the venture."

"You didn't say, Rufus, about today. You didn't say the old lady of the hill said something about today."

"What she said doesn't matter."

Remo was sure Rufus now regretted bringing it up. No matter. All their regrets would be settled shortly. The island smelled of the rich green health of its

23

plants. You could taste the plant oxygen in the air. Was that the plane? He didn't want to wait all night.

"What did she say about today, Rufus?"

"Not to worry your mind about it, mon. It will be a bit of all right."

"Rufus, you tell me now, or I am getting in the truck, my truck, and going back home with my truck. I'll leave you and your goods here on the cliff, a good day's walk back to the city."

"She said all would be well, friend."

"You're lying."

"All right, mon. I tell you the truth now and you'll run like a baby girl."

"I am not a coward. Talk."

Nice going, Rufus, thought Remo. He hated it when he had to go after one here and another there. He liked them kept together. Keep 'em together by pride, Rufus baby. Like the Marines.

"Well, friend, the old lady said that should we go on today's venture, we will meet a force from the east, kinda like what they call an Eastern god, against whom no single man can stand. Is what she said, all right."

There was laughter near the truck. Remo felt good.

"Oh, Rufus. You are a bit of a joker, aren't you. Hah, hah."

"I mean it, mon. She said we're gonna see something fearsome. A mon so fast no mon can see him."

The other man laughed also.

"Well, I'm glad to see you're not scared," came Rufus' voice. "I'm glad to see my quid went for nothing for the reading. She came up with the black stone of death over the green stones of life, she did. You can wager that one, mon."

The laughter subsided. The sound got louder. The single-engine Beechcraft, on its precarious way from

24

Mexico, would be landing soon. The pilot and its passenger had made a little mistake. They had made the kind of mistake one does not make if one intends to continue to successfully import heroin. They talked.

Oh, the conversation was casual and it was just a tentative offer to sell. But from that tentative offer to sell came the place. Then someone else deduced the time, the little plane was seen taking off and it was all put together into a telephone call, so here was Remo Williams sunning himself, listening to the soothing, sing-song talk of the Islands.

Here was Remo Williams, trained for nearly a decade as no Westerner had ever been trained, to do one thing better that any Westerner ever did before. To kill. With his hands. With his mind. With his body. Trained until he became something else.

Here was a planeload of men thinking the heroin they carried would get them maybe five to ten years if they had a bad lawyer or failed to buy favor from a judge. That is, if they were caught.

Well, there were other organizations, besides the courts, that dealt with crime. Organizations that thought maybe it was better that someone who imports heroin shouldn't. Organizations that thought that it was better that an importer die than a child.

All of which boiled down to upstairs telling Remo they wanted a simple heroin pop. Only with this heroin pop, you didn't pop your skin, you popped a supplier. Remo had been making these random pops for almost a year now. In between the big assignments. Like reading stupid geology books. He had been told that was a big assignment.

Remo watched the Beechcraft enlarge from a dot to a winged vehicle, going low over the Caribbean to decrease chances of detection. Must be a good navigator. No circling, just an approach. Remo looked at the plane to get the where and the feel of the men in it. Just staring at the white plane bobbing in the wind, an idea occurred to him; he felt immediately ashamed but intended to do it anyway.

He moved into the brush near the edge of the small clearing with the silence of a snake but the quickness of a cat. There he coiled. A small grunting toad made its way in front of his nose, then squatted, contemplating its relationship to the earth. The plane bobbed in, touched wheels, then up, then touched wheels again.

And Remo was off, the center of his body moving forward like a line drive to center field, his feet barely touching the sun-dried grass, only skimming it, until his hands reached the tail of the plane and he was running behind the plane, hands on its tail, feet skimming the ground.

The fumes from the engine up front whipped his face. He lowered the tail as he stayed with the bobbing, bouncing plane. Up ahead at the far end of the field, only about forty yards away now, was the truck and the three men. The pilot cut the engine and began applying the brakes. But as Remo pushed down on the tail hard, the nose of the plane bobbed up again, lifting the wheels and making the brakes useless. Then the front of the plane hit again and Remo bobbed it up again, and then just a slight push of the tail to the left, making the plane go right. It was really very easy and he guided the front of the plane into the truck, catching one man with the propeller. The other two were now attempting to aim their guns. From the inside of the cockpit, Remo heard two French voices shrieking. He imagined the pilot was being sworn at.

He would save the contents of the plane for last. Remo skipped behind the right wing of the plane. A young man in white shirt and trousers lay on the ground aiming a carbine at his groin. Remo bounded around the wingtip in a smooth motion, then came down on the man from behind, driving a thumb through the man's eye and into his brain.

Another man in whites dropped his rifle and stared disbelieving. He did this for only a fraction of a second since one cannot disbelieve for very long when one undergoes a frontal lobotomy, performed with the driving shards of one's own skull, propelled by a short, unseeable, knuckle blow to the head. The propeller had done less damage.

Remo snapped open the cockpit door above him and was in the cockpit in one motion. One man was still yelling in French at the pilot. Both carried light submachine guns strapped to their laps. Their guns stayed strapped to their laps, which was more than their heads did to their necks.

"Welcome, our French friends, bringing joy for needles," Remo said. The passenger, who was nearer to Remo, had a well-manicured Van Dyke. It was destinguished and gray. Then it was red. The deep perceptive gray eyes became red also. They were where the man used to do his seeing, before Remo loosened his spinal column at the neck.

Remo saw the pilot's eyes widen as he watched the slashing hands butcher his passenger's face.

"It's right behind the seat. You can have all of it. I will fly you anywhere Monsieur. Anywhere."

"You're only saying that because you love me," Remo said and gave the pilot's head a healthy little snap. So much for the plane. Then back outside to where the man lay in pain from the propeller goring.

His hair was graying and Remo could see he was facing death with nobility, a strength that could only make a man think of royalty.

He could barely speak. But he gasped, "You are the one the old lady predicted, are you not?"

Reno shrugged. "Maybe next time, if you pay for advice, you'll take it."

"You are the one."

"And you must be Rufus. I was listening to you."

"No. I am not Rufus, mon. Rufus is dead."

"Oh, gee, fella, I'm sorry. I didn't want you to think I thought you all looked alike. I mean I'm not insensitive."

"I am beyond pain."

"Okay," said Remo, cheerily. "So long." And he finished him with a simple blow to the temple.

Then he set fire to the plane and almost got knocked on his duff when the gasoline exploded. He hadn't really felt like searching for the heroin so why not burn it? It would go.

Despite everything, he was annoyed with himself. The business with the plane was foolish. It had not been the simplest point of attack; and as Chiun, his trainer, had told him many times:

"You will always be a white man. You play games."

Remo thought about that on the run back to the hotel. He needed a good run, not having had a really good workout for over a week.

# CHAPTER FOUR

The two girls watched the fat sheriff stumble up the slight hill with the plastic bag. The cool breeze made the far-off sunrise in the east a melody of red light to be enjoyed in comfort. It was fun watching Wyatt make his way along the rocky trail.

"If we gave him some," said one of the girls, "It'd probably kill him now."

"Then I feel like giving him some."

They sat stretched beneath a poplar tree, rubbing their bare feet into the soil. Wyatt reached the top of the hill puffing.

"It's all here. Feinstein's giving us trouble."

"Nobody gives us trouble," one girl said. "They give you trouble. They don't give us trouble."

Wyatt dropped the bag and fought for breath.

"Feinstein is giving him trouble," one girl told the other.

"Piggy always has trouble with liberals," the second girl said.

"Don't laugh, girls ... I mean, women. He's going to squeal to the feds in Washington."

"Then shoot him."

"Add another notch to your gun," the second girl said.

"I can't just shoot him."

"Well, how else would you kill someone, pig?"

"Piggy, piggy, pig, pig. Piggy's afraid to shoot his big bad gun."

"Is all the money there?" the first girl asked.

"Yeah. But Feinstein's going to Washington to squeal."

"Well, stop him somehow. You've got all these notches on your gun for something."

"I can't kill him," Wyatt said.

"Then we're going to have to," one of the girls said.

"That's murder," Wyatt said.

"So's Vietnam."

"We could go to the gas chamber for murder," Wyatt said.

"You can be killed walking across the street, piggy."

"That quake thing ... could it really snap off the entire fault? Could California go into the Pacific?" Wyatt asked.

"You can't make an omelette without breaking eggs, Piggy."

"Can you control it?" Wyatt inquired.

"Worry, you pig bastard. Worry."

"I'm worrying."

"Good. You should," said both girls in unison. Then they outlined what Sheriff Wyatt should do about Feinstein. And they told him what they would do when Feinstein got back.

"Do you have to?" asked Wyatt.

"Do you want to go to jail?"

"Maybe you could poison him or stab him or something?" Wyatt said.

The girls shook their heads.

"He really isn't such a bad guy," Wyatt said. "I mean, not that bad."

Then they divided the money. Wyatt got one

tenth. But he was assured he would get a hundred times that when things really got going.

"I wouldn't do this just for the money," said Wyatt.

"Then give the money back, piggy," one of the girls said.

Wyatt didn't.

# CHAPTER FIVE

Later that day, Harris Feinstein kept the appointment he had been able to wangle with the assistant secretary of the Department of the Interior. He found out that the assistant secretary had examined his case and forwarded it to the proper department.

*What department was that?* asked Feinstein.

*The Federal Bureau of Investigation,* answered the woman.

Feinstein checked in at a hotel. He had not planned on staying the evening. The next morning, he went to FBI headquarters. Yes, they had received a referral from the Interior Department but could not make heads or tails of it. Some cheating on insurance?

*No,* said Harris Feinstein. And he was questioned about his background and asked about troubles with his wife.

*What troubles?* Feinstein asked.

"Sheriff Wyatt back in San Aquino says you've been having troubles with your wife lately and he'd appreciate it and the whole town would appreciate it if we would not hold any funny talk against you. We have checked with several leading citizens and they all vouch that you are harmless. I'm afraid, Mr. Feinstein, your friends are worried that you might get hurt. There are some excellent doctors in Washington.

You might want to see one here if you're embarrassed to see one in San Aquino."

And so Harris Feinstein did not detail how California and the rest of the country, for that matter, might soon be at the hands of insane blackmailers with the power to create earthquakes whenever they wanted. Instead, he went back to the Department of the Interior and started to yell at the man who had transferred him to the FBI in the first place.

He yelled, although he knew his yelling corroborated the rumors of his insanity. He yelled, although he knew he was getting nowhere. He yelled because, dammit, he wanted to yell and the Department of the Interior was made up of idiots. If they weren't idiots in the first place, they wouldn't be in the Department of the Interior.

"If you'll listen to me," said the assistant something or other, Feinstein was not quite sure assistant to or of what, "you'd find that we do have someone interested in what you're talking about. His name is Silas McAndrew. He's on the street level floor. Here's his room number."

The assistant something or other handed Harris Feinstein a slip of paper. Feinstein left the office and walked down the long, incredibly long, corridors of the Department of the Interior. It was as if someone had designed the building to cow its visitors. Harris Feinstein was not about to be cowed.

It took him twenty-five minutes of following what he was sure was a non-system numbering system before he reached the number on the slip. He knocked.

"Come in," came the voice of Eastern nasality.

Harris Feinstein entered. He saw a small office with a bare lightbulb burning furiously yellow above. He saw stacks of papers and cartons piled up, some of them twelve feet high. But he did not see the person who invited him in.

"I'm here," came a voice from behind a large paper carton which seemed about to surrender to an expansion of manila folders. "I'm Silas McAndrew."

Harris Feinstein looked around the carton. There was a man hunched over a typewriter, his jacket sprawled on his desk, his tie open, his shirt sleeves rolled up. He wore thick glasses. He smiled.

"No secretary." Then he offered his hand. It was a good handshake, not nervously strong or disengagingly weak. A solid, normal handshake with a very nice smile.

"I'm Harris Feinstein. I suppose you've heard of me from assistant whatever he is."

"Oh," said the young man with the honest, open face. "No, I haven't."

"Why did you say 'oh'?"

"Because I know why you're here. Sit down."

"Thank God," said Feinstein, looking for a place to sit and settling for the top of a very large boulder. At least it looked like a boulder. Or a piece of one. It was not dirty, however.

"Okay," said Harris Feinstein. "What are we going to do?"

"Well, first tell me why you're here."

"You said you knew why I was here?"

Silas McAndrew lowered his eyes to his typewriter. "Uh, yeah. Let me straighten that out for you, Mr. Feinstein. I'm sort of the department that handles the unusual cases and what I meant by I know why you're here, was I know upstairs didn't exactly get along with you, right?"

"Oh," said Feinstein.

"But go ahead. Tell me your story. I'm all ears. Maybe I can help you."

"I hope so, but I doubt it," said Feinstein. He

glanced briefly out the dusty window which rested on a humming air conditioner and then he began, sometimes looking down at his shoes, sometimes out the dusty window at sweltering Washington, sometimes just looking off, out into space somewhere, because he was sure he would meet another rebuff. What he was saying was that there was a real threat to America.

His story didn't take very long.

"So that's it. You can now file me away under assorted cranks and nuts. And thank you."

Harris Feinstein began to rise, until he felt a hand on his arm. Silas McAndrew stared at him, a piercing, questioning gaze. McAndrew looked different from when Feinstein had first entered the office. Now his well-tanned face had whitened and the probing showed fear.

"Don't go, Mr. Feinstein. Continue."

"Well, that's it."

"Not quite, Mr. Feinstein," McAndrew said. "You know, I'm a geologist. I get the geology and environment nuts. I wish you were one of them. I desperately wish you were. But I don't think so. Fact is, I believe you."

"Why should you? Nobody else did."

"Because I am a geologist," McAndrew said. "I don't have to tell you that California is earthquake country. Every year, the earthquakes number in the tens of thousands. Sure, mostly small and no damage, but all recordable. One of the things we do around here, Mr. Feinstein, is keep a map of where earthquakes occur. You've seen them. Pointy pins pressed into a map. In the last year or so, the frequencies all seem to have changed. I've been wondering why for the past six months. Now I know. Someone's been tampering with nature. Someone's been experimenting."

The telephone rang. McAndrew reached a hand

toward the noise which came from under a pile of magazines.

"Hello," McAndrew said. Then he tilted the receiver away from his ear slightly so that Feinstein could hear the conversation.

"Yes, Sheriff Wyatt. Yes. Has he been here? Yes. Why do you ask?"

Wyatt's voice came over the phone smooth and very calm. It shocked Harris Feinstein how intelligent long distance could make Wade Wyatt sound.

"Well, frankly, Mr. McAndrew, we were worried about Mr. Feinstein out here in San Aquino. He's one of our leading citizens and best loved, too. He's a very sensitive person and belongs to many charitable organizations. I hope this will go no further, Mr. McAndrew, but he's become disturbed over earthquakes. Very deeply. He thinks that they're part of a plot and that someone controls them. Now he's trying to get other people to think that way. I don't know what he told you, whether he's talked to God. Did he tell you that?"

"No."

"Well, he feels obliged to save the world from earthquakes. It's an assignment from God, he says. I've spoken to the FBI, Mr. McAndrew. It's not that he's dangerous. And if you could spare the effort, I and a lot of people here in San Aquino would appreciate it if you would humor him. Sort of pretend that you are going to investigate. I know that will help him and perhaps he'll return then to his wife. He's had trouble at home."

"I see," said Silas McAndrew, looking over his clear rimless glasses at the gentleman from California. "Perhaps you would suggest our even investigating whatever he suggests. We could send some men to San Aquino to look around. They won't know they're not

37

on a real mission. They'll go through it, just like it was all for real."

"Oh, no," Wyatt said. "That won't be necessary. You don't have to go that far."

"Why not?" said McAndrew, his Ohio face calm as the Miami River on a flat hot July day.

"Well, it isn't necessary, that's all."

"We've got to investigate something. We'll investigate his earthquake thing." McAndrew saw a smile grow on Feinstein's face.

There was a pause and a slight hint of muffling as if a hand had been put over the phone. Then: "Sure, fine, that'll be great. We think it's really wonderful. I mean, I really think that's fine that you'll go so far to humor a sick man. Thanks very much. So long."

"Goodbye."

To Feinstein, McAndrew said: "Somebody's got brains back there."

"You Easterners are pretty sharp," said Feinstein. "I've known Wyatt all my life and I believed right up until the end of the phone conversation he had hidden his brains from me."

"Yeah. A lot of brains out there. If I had gotten that call before you came in, I would have treated you like you were treated everyplace else in Washington. I'm from Ohio, by the way."

"That's what I said," said Harris Feinstein. "An Easterner."

Before they left his office, Silas McAndrew typed a routine memo which might very well have represented his and Harris Feinstein's last gift to the United States. They would never be able to make another, not after they flew back to California and made the mistake of discussing that State's problems with an eccentric scientist and his two extraordinary assistants.

# CHAPTER SIX

When Sheriff Wade Wyatt saw the bodies in the Cowboy Motel on the mountain road highway just outside San Aquino, he said, "Oh, sweet Jesus, God have mercy, no."

Then he reeled out of the motel suite into the men's room in the lobby, where he vomited into a urinal, and kept flushing and upchucking and seeing his lunch collect on the large white mothball cube in red and white splotches, evidence that he had not yet learned to chew.

"No," he said, keeping his hand on the flusher. "No. He was in Washington, just yesterday. No."

"Yes," said his young deputy. "Should I call the county coroner?"

"Yeah. The coroner. Sure."

"And the town police. The motel's always been kinda half county, half town anyway."

"No," Wyatt said. "No town police. We'll take care of it."

"Should I get a photographer?"

"Yeah. Good move. A photographer."

"They sure look bad, the two of them, don't they, sheriff?"

"Yeah. Bad."

"What do you think killed 'em?"

Sheriff Wyatt did not answer. He knew who and

what had killed them and he was terrified. His head had returned to the urinal. Now he was breathing the freshness of the cold running water near his head, almost a chlorine freshness.

"You going back in the room, sheriff?"

Wyatt caught his breath. "Yeah. Got to."

"They sure look bad, as if they was grabbed by two giant hands that just popped 'em open, like squeezing a grape. Pow!"

Sheriff Wyatt went to the sink and steadied himself. His eyes had reddened. His hands trembled. He washed his face with cold water, then dried it with the paper towels provided by the Cowboy Motel, the only motel in San Aquino County with massage beds and headboard electric outlets for any device you might want to plug in. Batteries were sold at the front desk.

He glanced at the young deputy in the mirror. His mouth was moving.

"You eating something?" asked Wyatt.

"No. Just sucking on a Mary Jane."

"You get outta here, boy, before I bust you. Get out."

Sheriff Wyatt brushed his crewcut with his hands as he heard the door slam. He replaced the Stetson he had parked on the top of the urinal and strode back into the lobby, ordering people back into their rooms, saying everything was under control.

The motel owner was standing by the suite when Wyatt reached it.

"Stay out. My deputy will have questions for you."

"Uh, sheriff. I don't know how to say this, but, you know, I recognize one of the victims. They didn't pay in advance. They had American Express and now there's no one to sign."

40

"What do you want from me? He's one of your kind."

"I'm Armenian," the owner said.

"That's Jew, ain't it?"

"No. You see. . . ."

"You look Jew."

"I'm not."

"Tough titty, baby, 'cause you sure look it. Now you stay outside of this suite. I'm going in. You see the bodies?"

"Yes."

"Pretty horrible, huh?"

"When there's no one to sign, it's very horrible. You see the Cowboy Motel is a marginal business. . . ."

Sheriff Wyatt shut the door behind him. And there they were on the bed with the massager still running. Both of them naked, like two fruits. Who would have thought it of Feinstein? Sure, Sheriff Wyatt called him faggy, but not faggy like that. Not faggy nude in bed with the young fellow who according to the ID card was Silas McAndrew, a geologist for the Department of the Interior. The fellow Wyatt had talked to the day before.

Sheriff Wyatt kept focusing on the knees and groins to keep from looking at their mouths. He didn't want to look at their mouths or their heads. He looked at the water that soaked the bed near the men's waists, and then his eyes strayed up to their heads and he ran from the room again.

What he had seen was two men with their intestines squeezed out through their mouths, like they had choked on their own stomachs, dark red balloon organs squeezed like toothpaste from the bowels of their bodies.

He had been warned there could be deaths like

that. One could even await him. But he hadn't really believed it. Not until now.

Wyatt lurched into the men's room again and made it to the urinal but there was nothing left and he just stood there, leaning into the flowing water. Naturally, he had parked his Stetson on top of the plunger before surrendering to his stomach.

The bathroom door opened again and the deputy came in mumbling something about looking for the sheriff again because the photographer was here to get the pictures of the two bodies.

"Go ahead. Take 'em."

"Should I question the owner too for a report?"

"Yeah."

"Then remove the bodies, sheriff?"

"Yeah. Bodies."

Sheriff Wyatt gasped for air.

"Sheriff?"

"Yeah?"

"Uh, some of the fellows just got a bag from Binky Burger and we got an extra goulash here with sloppy joe sauce if you want it."

"Get the bodies out of the motel," said Sheriff Wyatt, who did not fire his deputy on the spot only because he was too weak to do so.

Out in the San Aquino sun, looking down the hillside at the rising spruce and the valley beyond that and the mountains beyond that, with the homes dotted here and there, clean and fresh and sprawling, not cramped like some other places, Sheriff Wyatt regained his breath and his composure, then ambled across the gravel shoulder to his official car parked there. Even on an investigation, he would not park the official car in front of the Cowboy Motel lest there be nothing there to investigate and someone should later remember seeing the red bubble and the sheriff's gold stars on the black and white Plymouth. Then the rumors.

Rumors could kill an elected official.

Sheriff Wyatt plopped himself into his front seat, drew another breath, then drove to the offices of the First Aquino Trust and Development Corporation, Lester Curpwell IV, President, marched across the neat conservative gray rug, past the two secretaries with their polished wood desks, and into a panelled office where he waited for Lester Curpwell IV.

Curpwell was there in five minutes.

"Harris Feinstein is dead," Wyatt said as soon as Curpwell entered.

Curpwell sat at the brown leather chair behind his wide desk, without looking up, just staring vacantly at the desk. He sat under a larger-than-life-sized portrait of the first Curpwell, and like the portrait, said nothing.

Wyatt fingered his Stetson some more. He shifted his weight.

"Oh, no," said Curpwell, bleakly. "What happened?"

"Damned if I know. Harris and this guy from the Interior Department were found about twenty-five minutes ago, dead in the Cowboy." Sheriff Wyatt did not bother to say Cowboy Motel. Everyone knew the Cowboy was the Cowboy Motel. "Naked as the day they was born. I spoke to this McAndrew fellow just yesterday. He talked to Feinstein and I guess he came back with him for a look-see. Beats me why they came to the Cowboy to play fag games."

"Not a word of this must get in the papers," said Curpwell. "Have you notified Mrs. Feinstein?"

"Well, gee, not yet, Mr. Curpwell, I came here as soon as. . . ."

"Good, I'll do it."

43

"I don't know about the papers. There's been a lot of talk, a lot of people at the motel, and. . . ."

"You don't have to report he was found nude, with a man."

"No sir. He had the guts sucked outa him. Both of 'em."

"Is that how they died?"

"Must of. It was bad."

"In your coroner's report, you will have them ... have them. . . ." Lester Curpwell paused.

"Found in bed with women?"

"No. You'll have them die of ptomaine. Probably from a bad meal back in Washington."

"Shoot, no. I mean, you're a Curpwell and everything but I ain't going to commit no felony for you."

"You're going to do what you're told, Wade Wyatt, and now get out of here."

Sheriff Wade Wyatt stood for a moment in glum protest.

Then he got out of there.

# CHAPTER SEVEN

Silas McAndrew and Harris Feinstein had left a gift to America.

The gift was simply a memo to McAndrew's superior in the Department of the Interior. This was the chap who was always interested in anything unusual or in cases of corruption. He was the man who had asked for reports on the peculiarities out in California—specifically the geological ones.

The memo McAndrew wrote said he had corroborating evidence from a Harris Feinstein that indeed someone had found a way to tamper with nature to produce—or prevent—earthquakes. Not a hoax, McAndrew said. Could mean major scale destruction for the state. He was going to California. He meant to discuss the problem with a certain professor out there.

So that was the memo. The superior who had been curious about what was going on out there in California did not file the memo. He sent it along to the people who had told him what in general to look for and recently had expressed great interest in California geology. He didn't mind sending the material to the people who asked for it. They gave him $400 a month non-taxable spending money and arranged for him to be promoted faster than his colleagues.

He thought they were the FBI or the CIA or something.

McAndrew's superior did not know whom the information ultimately reached, for if he knew, that organization's main mission would have failed; a mission that had been given by a young President to an operative of the Central Intelligence Agency who quickly went on the retired list.

The mission was part confession. The United States Constitution did not work. To follow it meant chaos in the future. To abandon it meant a police state. Crime was winning, and so the young president created the new organization—CURE—a name never written on a memo and which only three Americans would ultimately know: The President, the chief of CURE, and the enforcement arm, a young former policeman named Remo Williams, who as the legend grew, came to be known by the Oriental name, Shiva, "The Destroyer."

What the Constitution could not do, CURE did. Quietly. Evidence from bribed witnesses would suddenly and mysteriously be changed. A judge who owed a political debt to a corrupt machine would discover he owed a greater debt to his secret mistress and she demanded a fair verdict. Information on government corruption would accidentally be leaked to a newspaper by a man who had a second salary.

A Mafia don, armored with money and influence, would hear a curtain rustle but never even see the hand that smashed his skull.

An enforcer for a crime syndicate would suddenly disappear.

The wave of crime, corruption and chaos that seemed ready to engulf the giant young democracy subsided and started to meet setbacks. The Constitution survived.

In Rye, New York, on the third floor of Folcroft Sanitarium, overlooking Long Island Sound, a thin, lemon-faced man looked over McAndrews' last memo. Then he dialed a phone number. It would take four minutes to complete because a route check on that line would disclose that a bakery in Duluth, not Folcroft Sanitarium, was making the call to the Caribbean.

When the call was completed, Dr. Harold Smith, director of Folcroft and director of CURE, heard the line buzz. Then the receiver was lifted.

"Hello," Smith said. "Vacation's over."

On the other end of the phone, fifteen hundred miles away, in a Caribbean hotel room, Remo Williams felt very, very good. Vacations were boring. It would be good to work again.

# CHAPTER EIGHT

Harris Feinstein was buried before the Lord God of Israel, King of the Universe and the leading citizens of San Aquino. Most citizens of San Aquino wondered why the casket was not opened.

Presumably, the King of the Universe knew.

So did Sheriff Wade Wyatt and Lester Curpwell IV.

The rabbi, a man of fine sensitive features who had just been graduated from the seminary, somehow or other got the Vietnamese war into Harris Feinstein's death.

Mrs. Feinstein shot him a dirty look. The rabbi ignored her. Sheriff Wyatt shot everyone a dirty look. Everyone ignored him. Les Curpwell stood with his head bowed.

Wyatt kept looking around to see if he could spot anyone he knew, maybe wanted on a charge of something or other. He didn't.

The rabbi defined what a good man meant. He defined what a good life was. He defined what thousands of years of study had decided was a good life and a good death.

Sheriff Wyatt thought that sounded okay, depending on how you interpreted the rabbi's sentiments.

In the last calling to the creator of all that is, was, and ever will be, the rabbi's voice rose over Beth

49

Shalom Cemetery into the clear California sky. Its ancient, vibrant cadences were part of the meaning of the Universe.

And the ground everyone stood on most certainly would have done proud the scribes of the Old Testament. The ground they stood on was preparing—unless someone could be stopped—to give up the dead buried therein, and to cast into the Pacific Ocean multitudes upon multitudes of people, to bury cities alive, to crush millions, to lay waste human and animal life as only an earth upheaval could do.

If a scribe with a knowing historical eye had been at the Feinstein funeral, he might have written:

"And thus the elder Feinstein of two score and fourteen years was put to ground. And around him were his friends and family. And they did not know what the earth had stored for them, neither did they know the birds of the trees, or the moles of the ground who knew the tremors of the earth.

"Men slept with women to whom marriage was not given and young women freely of themselves gave. Gluttony was upon the land and men in leisure would not walk but sat on cushioned chairs, their comfort to bestow.

"Men with men did intercourse conduct and women in all unclean things, then did the people of this land indulge. Brother against brother took up arms, poor against rich, black against white, Gentile and Hebrew alike did nourish these hatreds in their souls.

"And none looked to the Lord God of all mankind whose sweetness had brought such bounty. None looked, for even their cemeteries told them that this world and the next was for their comfort alone.

"Only some voices warned: 'Repent, repent, repent.' But they were scorned and rebuked for their truth and driven from there with oaths and profanities."

"Get those fucking coocoos outa this here funeral. Jesus Christ, can't those dingaling dingbats see there's a fucking funeral going on here."

Thus bespake Sheriff Wyatt.

Thus to the cemetery gate were five young hippies escorted by deputies.

The funeral services stopped. Everyone stared at Sheriff Wyatt.

"Sorry," he said, grinning sheepishly and removing his Stetson. "I guess I talked a bit loud. Oh. Sorry again. The hat stays on. Heh, heh."

\* \* \*

It was not announced at the funeral, but a man named Remo something-or-other had purchased, through an agent, the Feinstein Department Store. The Feinstein home also had been sold to him, but what his name was, Mrs. Feinstein didn't remember. Mrs. Feinstein was leaving San Aquino that day, because with her daughters married and now Harris gone, there were just too many good memories to see each day and her heart could not sustain her sweet bitterness.

At about the time the late Harris Feinstein's friends were discovering his store had been sold, its new owner was discovering what he had bought.

"A department store? Are you out of your head? I don't know anything about department stores."

Remo drummed his fingers lightly on the sun-heated dashboard of the rented car. He did not look at Dr. Harold W. Smith but stared straight ahead at the neat, manicured valley baking in the hot California summer sun. He had made the airport connection in

Los Angeles and had put his one valise in the trunk of the car Smith had rented. Chiun was being driven in a hired limousine behind them, barely big enough for his steamer trunks, television sets and taping devices.

"You don't need to know anything about department stores. The manager has been told to continue running the store until you are ready to get involved in its operation. Say, in two or three months. You'll have plenty of time. More than you need, since the plan is rather simple."

"It always is with my life."

"As you know, San Aquino has been asked to pay earthquake insurance, $8,000 a month. You are assuming Feinstein's position in the town. You'll be asked to participate. Play it by ear from then on, but try to give the earthquake people some grief. And when they come after you. . . ." He didn't finish the sentence. Instead, he said: "This could easily and quickly become a national catastrophe. If the earthquake people decide to branch out. Or if something annoys them and they trigger a major earthquake. It could be the greatest tragedy in our history."

"Second greatest," Remo said.

"What's the first?"

"When man came down out of the trees," said Remo Williams.

"Be serious. Why do you think we sent you that geology tutor? We've been watching this thing for a couple of months. And we haven't been able to get a handle on who or what. And now, with Feinstein and McAndrew dead, it makes it a different ball-game. The earthquake people will kill."

"How do you know there really is somebody behind this?" Remo said. "Maybe a coincidence."

"No," Smith said. "The earthquake frequencies are

off all over the State These people can cause quakes and they can prevent them. And that makes them dangerous. Too dangerous to live."

"You have great faith in my success."

"How much did you absorb about geology?," Smith asked.

"Not much," Remo said.

"Well, there's an outfit in this county called the Richter Institute. It's headed by a man named Dr. Silas Forben. They call him "Dr. Quake." He's had a screw loose for a couple of years but he probably knows more about earthquakes than any other man alive. McAndrew and Feinstein were planning to see him. If you need to know anything about quakes, ask him."

"Maybe he's the earthquake maker?," Remo said.

"Maybe," Smith said. He did not sound convinced. "Keep me posted on what you find out. It may be that we'll want to send geologists out here, if it's something scientific. And you may have to take care of them, too, when they're done with their work."

"You never change, Dr. Smith."

"You're not exactly an innocent yourself, Remo."

"I never asked for this job. I was framed for murder, remember. I was electrocuted, damn near, remember. And I woke up in your neat little organization with the sonofabitch who framed me telling me America was worth a life. It was. His. Remember? I know the business. And I know you're a sonofabitch. And I know I'm a sonofabitch. It doesn't bother you, but it does bother me."

Remo stared straight ahead into the blooming California countryside, only he did not see the countryside. He stared into his hate.

"Chiun was supposed to work on that with you," said Smith.

"He didn't succeed. I'm an American."

"Well."

"Well, not your kind, obviously."

"I'm sorry," Smith said. "You're very good at what you do."

"That's the first compliment you've ever given me and I find it repulsive."

Soon, Smith reached a ranchhouse with a sprawling lawn, circular driveway and lovely Grecian pottery at the door. Cars were parked in the driveway. By the people standing around on the lawn with drinks in their hands, it looked as if a party were in progress.

"The funeral was supposed to be yesterday," Smith said.

"You mentioned something about lungs being forced out through the mouth?"

"A pressure killing," Smith said.

Remo found that very interesting. Then something dawned on him. "Why yesterday for the funeral? Why so soon?"

"Jews bury within twenty-four hours. I guess he was too badly mangled. Might have taken the coroner too long to determine the cause of death. Newspapers called it a case of accidental poisoning, so that is what you're supposed to believe. Oh, by the way," he said, slipping Remo a wallet that appeared worn but which Remo knew wasn't ever really used, lest it contain some trace, some small trace of where it had been before, "You're Remo Blomberg. You want to enter the department store business—retail, they call it.

"Your parents died young leaving you lots of money. You were raised by an Aunt Ethel in Miami Beach. You know the area a bit. Don't give your aunt's name and address. Just say you have an aunt. Don't worry about not going to temple or kosher eating habits. You're a Reformed Jew. Whenever

54

someone asks you for a donation, give, and no one will know you're not a Jew."

"I knew an Israeli agent once. Briefly."

"Different culture. Forget it."

Smith pulled into the driveway, and almost as if it were on signal, the people began to leave. "I guess they stopped here for a farewell drink," Smith said. "The house is yours and so's the store. Both paid in full. It's getting late and I'm going to have to leave. Here comes Chiun."

Smith stopped in front of the house and the rented limousine pulled up behind them. The driver jumped out and opened the back door for a frail Oriental in flowing green robes. He helped the elderly man to the front steps. Chiun thanked him politely. He took Chiun's three trunks from the back of the limousine and lugged them to the sidewalk, along with Chiun's television equipment. The driver motioned that Chiun might, if he wished, sit on the trunks. He helped the elderly man to sit down.

Remo shook his head. Chiun was playing helpless again. Chiun often did this to get people to carry his luggage or haul things from place to place. He did not bother to inform those who did the hauling that he could twist them like soft candy if he felt like it. Nor did he inform them that he was the Master of Sinanju, before whom all men were merely targets in motion.

Once when a woman was carrying Chiun's shopping packages and had lost the key to her locked car, Chiun had pressured the metal handle open. He explained that it had really been unlocked. But it took the garage a week to get another lock to replace the one Chiun had mangled.

Now Chiun again was playing helpless and basking

in the late afternoon sun of a California summer. He probably expected to be carried into the house.

Smith looked at his watch again and Remo removed his single valise from the back seat and hopped out of the car. As he turned, he saw that Chiun was no longer sitting on his trunks. He was in the driveway commiserating with a woman dressed all in black and he was bowing mournfully.

Remo looked up at the neat manicured lawn, and the people now leaving and wondered suddenly why people mourned death as if it were an accident befalling the unlucky, when every one of them would suffer the same inevitable fate.

And for these people, it could be soon, depending on how successful Remo was at his job. He saw seven dark birds take off from a popular tree in the distance, as though frightened by a cat. For all he knew that could be another low tremor. Birds could feel the tremors best.

How many earthquakes a year did California have? Little earth tremors. Little adjustments of the forces of the crust of the earth. Like bugs in a bottle that kids would cap, and maybe they'd remember to let in air. Maybe the little bugs would live.

They were all bugs in the bottle, only now the problem wasn't air. Someone was going to smash the bottle under foot. With all the human bugs in it.

# CHAPTER NINE

The well built homes were not damaged that night. Only the chandeliers swayed slightly. Barefoot, Remo could not feel it on the stone floor of the living room. Neither did Chiun stir and he slept on a mat on the floor of his bedroom.

Out across the lawn a cat howled, Remo looked to the blue-black sky with its lost moon, feeling very alone and very helpless, frightened to a degree that he had never felt since his training with Chiun had begun.

So he closed his eyes, closed his mind and for a moment was silent. When he opened his eyes he was calm again. *An over active mind is a dagger in one's own heart* was an old saying from the Korean village of Sinanju whence the master came.

Other homes were not so safe that night. They were not strong, they were not solid, they boasted no plumbing or air conditioning or central heating.

They were the homes of the grape pickers, the people who came to San Aquino in the spring and summer to work the vineyards, then who left after the late season harvest. Aquino grapes were good grapes, vermouth grapes for America's leading vermouth.

So while the owners of the vineyards did not really feel the quake that night, the pickers did. For the tremor that could sway a chandelier could collapse a sheet metal wall or sever a two-by-four nailed to another two-by-four that was supposed to hold up a roof.

Three shacks came down in the San Aquino night like houses of cards.

Bare light bulbs flicked on in the standing shacks. People in nightgowns and underdrawers, some in slacks and nothing else fled from their shacks, shrieking.

Lung-choking dust rose from the collection of tin and wooden rubble.

Someone yelled in Spanish.

"Men. We need men. Help."

A fat, bloodied hand reached its way out from under a splintered beam and in Spanish, a weak voice called from the direction of the hand: "Please. Please."

"Here. Help me with this beam," yelled one man in slacks and bare feet. It was cool, but his body was soaked wet as he struggled to lift a beam off the fat, moving arm with the bloodied hand.

From one pile of sheet metal and wood and tarpaper came a baby's cry.

It cried as men peeled off strips of housing with their hands. It cried when the cranes and tractors arrived from the town of San Aquino. No one standing around the shacks could stop it or pick it up or comfort it, and the men working to untangle the pile felt helpless, afraid and angry at the building that did not yield fast enough and the child they could not find fast enough.

In the middle of the night, the crying stopped and when the dead baby's body was discovered in a little artificial womb made by the accident of a beam fall-

58

ing onto a table—the grape pickers of San Aquino returned to their shacks in silence.

And they did not go to the fields the next day, although the sun was high and hot, and in the words of generations of migrants, it was "weather to work."

"Jeez," mumbled Sheriff Wade Wyatt. "Spooky wetback labor. Anything'll spook 'em."

He had arrived on the scene in the morning, having discovered by telephone the previous night that no white men had been killed and having therefore returned to sleep.

"Won't go to the fields, huh?," asked Wyatt of the owner of the Gromucci ranch. "Shoot. You think it's the Commies stirring them up?"

"No," said Robert Gromucci, the owner. Gromucci leaned from the window of his pink Eldorado convertible and looked up to Sheriff Wyatt taking notes.

"Seven people were killed last night," Gromucci said.

"All greasers though—right?"

"All Mexican-Americans."

"Seven. The shacks went?"

"Your deputy has the report."

"Yeah, sure. I just wanted to get some of the details of the quake."

"The workers are restless today," Gromucci said.

"In the old days we knew how to handle that, Bob, but I can't do anything for you today. You know my hands are tied."

"I wasn't asking you to work them over, Wade. They're talking about this being the year of the big curse or something. The gods of the earth versus the gods of destruction. I don't know."

"I thought you people believed in that stuff too, Bob. No offense."

"No," said Robert Gromucci, owner of Gromucci

Farms. "We don't. You look unusually content this morning, Wade."

Which was true. Wade Wyatt had warned the San Aquino committee—Curpwell and Rucker and Boydenhousen—that the quake would be coming. Reprisal for Feinstein's trip to Washington. Reprisal for Washington sending in McAndrew. Warning not to make any more trips or to welcome any more federal men.

"No, no more than usual, Bob," Wyatt said. "It's just that good old, uneducated hick, redneck Wade Wyatt isn't always wrong, you know, and sometimes he has a right to gloat."

"Seven people are dead, Wade."

"So, hire others. I'll see you, Bob. Take care. Regards to the missus," yelled Wyatt, trotting backwards as he talked.

He entered his star-studded Plymouth and wheeled the vehicle onto the dusty road out of the camp and to the highway which was coming alive with the morning San Aquino traffic.

Wyatt whistled pleasantly as he drove down the mountain highway, past the Cowboy Motel, with its occupants entering their cars, many without luggage. Then past the string of used-car lots and car washes, and then the Aquino shopping center dominated by the Feinstein Department store.

He wondered if the new owner would change the name of the store to Blomberg's. Or maybe Remo's. The guy seemed regular enough but one could never tell with those kind of people. Take his Oriental servant, for instance. It was real obvious the man was no servant. He didn't have enough energy to even take his bags into the house. Sheriff Wyatt, who had driven up to the house, had ordered his deputy to do that.

Come to think of it, the new owner was obviously as queer as a pink banana. Why else have that old Oriental there? He was no servant. Too weak. Probably be dead in a month.

Could those little gooks be beating us in Vietnam? No. Sheriff Wyatt knew who was beating America in Nam. America was beating America in Nam.

But Sheriff Wyatt was a politician too. And as he pulled into the diner near the Curpwell building, he vowed that like his feelings on Vietnam and who was really responsible, he would keep his feelings about Remo Blomberg to himself. Bottled up.

The coffee in the Andropolos Diner was good that morning. Black and bitter and when meshed with globs of sugar from the spoon and swilled with cream—the real stuff, not what Andropolos served his regular customers—it tasted rich and good and solid.

"Pie ala mode. Cherry pie with vanilla fudge, Gertie," said Sheriff Wyatt to the counter girl. She was in her late thirties, the hardening result of too many one-night stands with too many customers who asked what she was doing when she got off that night, and too many "nothing muches."

She was Gertie and they told Gertie dirty jokes and she laughed at them. And they pinched Gertie and Gertie might get mad but Gertie getting mad didn't really count because she was Gertie.

Gertie was the woman who heard all the latest smut.

Gertie was also the waitress at Andropolos' who received the highest tips. And Gertie, as Sheriff Wyatt knew, had one hell of a bank account.

Sheriff Wyatt's ham buttocks crowned the red vinyl counter stool, smothering it in khaki-clad flesh that almost hid the stool top.

He rested his elbows on the counter and burped. Gertie brought him the pie ala mode.

"Heard seven people were killed out at Gromucci's last night," Gertie said. "A baby too. One of the men said that the kid kept crying throughout the whole thing. The whole night. And then it stopped and when they found it, it was dead. It was a girl. Her mother and her father were killed, too. One of her brothers. Only three kids out of that family lived. Those shacks are a disgrace, you know, Wade."

"Look," said Wyatt, his beefy face reddening. "I'm gonna eat this pie. And I'm gonna eat this ice cream. But next time when I order cherry pie ala mode with vanilla fudge, I want cherry pie with vanilla fudge. Not vanilla ripple."

Sheriff Wyatt plunged the fork into the vanilla ripple, its prongs making even tunnels through the white and brown ice cream.

"You're a bit much, Wade."

Sheriff Wyatt waved the fork in front of Gertie's face, far enough away, however, to avoid any contact with her makeup. Then he would have to get another fork.

"I'll tell you, this may be the third time this year that I've ordered vanilla fudge and gotten vanilla ripple."

"What about the people who were killed, Wade?"

"Serving me ripple instead of fudge ain't gonna bring 'em back."

"You ain't paying for it."

"I'll pay for it. Bring me fudge."

"We're out. You want another flavor?"

"No. Ripple will do."

Gertie, unwounded by combat, stayed near Wyatt. "They say the wetbacks are talking about death. A lot of it. That they may go back home. That they got their warnings," said Gertie.

Sheriff Wyatt drained his cup. "Good riddance. Whole pack of 'em."

"Who'll pick the grapes?"

"Americans."

"At those wages?"

"Then they'll get machines. Machines don't stink like wetbacks. You can park a machine in a garage. The machine don't want to move in with you or go to the movies with you. Machines'll take orders too."

"Not nowadays," laughed Gertie.

Sheriff Wyatt laughed too.

"That new fellow who bought Feinstein's?" Gertie said.

"Remo Blomberg?"

"Yeah. I saw him this morning on my way to work."

"At five A.M.?"

"Yeah," Gertie said. "He was out on his lawn doing the damnedest exercises I ever saw."

"Yeah?"

"Yeah. It was like crazy. I mean, it was dark, so I can't be sure, but it was like he was running fast. Real fast. Faster than I ever saw anybody run. And then it would be like he hit a wall, he changed directions so fast. Like he did it without his legs. Like the cartoons or the old movies. He'd be zipping along here, then zipping along there, then *pow*, he'd be going somewhere else. Weirdest thing I ever saw.

"And then," she said, "then he lay down on the ground and it was like he was vibrating or something. Then he did the strangest thing I've ever seen. I mean *ever*. I mean, I've been to the Cowboy and all and I mean ever. He's laying face down on the lawn, and then he's in the air, flipping over backwards. Like a cat. I mean it."

Gertie played nervously with her counter-rag, twisting it and watching Sheriff Wyatt's eyes closely as she told her story.

Wyatt offered his cup for more coffee. Gertie reached behind her to the constantly-heated carafe and poured it. Wyatt added the sugar and real cream.

"What do you think about that?" Gertie asked.

Wyatt beckoned her closer with his fork. He had a bit of information for her.

"He's queer. Fagola. Probably doing ballet."

"No kidding?" said Gertie, shocked. "I'd never believe it."

"You can believe it."

"No kidding," repeated Gertie, quite satisfied with what she had gleaned. She paused. "You know, I know and most of the town knows what really happened at the motel with Feinstein and the other guy. Yeah, I know poisoning and all. It really happened at the motel, naked and all. But they weren't queer, in case you thought so. I know. The two of 'em were with broads."

"No."

"Yeah," Gertie said. "They were doing a real gang number with a bunch of broads."

"In the Cowboy?"

"You know it."

"No."

"Yeah," said Gertie conspiratorially. "With a bunch of broads."

"Oh," said Wyatt dumbly and dropped his fork to his plate. "I didn't know that."

He waited in the diner until he saw Lester Curpwell's silver Rolls Royce pull up in front of the Curpwell building. Let Gertie think whatever she wanted, he told himself, as he shouted and crossed the street. Wyatt knew how the two men had died. By whose hand. And he didn't like it.

He caught up with Curpwell just in front of the main door.

"I've got to speak with you right away," he said. "Last night was a warning. The earthquake people called me. There are some things we've got to do."

"One thing we've got to do," Curpwell said, "is not talk out here on the street. We'll talk this afternoon. I think it's time that Mr. Remo Blomberg learned about the expenses of owning Feinstein's."

# CHAPTER TEN

Sheriff Wyatt himself went to pick up the new owner of Feinstein's. The store had remained open under the vice president's charge, and the new owner had yet to appear there. Curpwell had invited Remo Blomberg himself over the telephone. Wyatt was told to be friendly to sort of let the new man know he was among friends in San Aquino.

Sheriff Wyatt was tired, bone tired, as he drove up the curved driveway to the Feinstein house. Funny. He still thought of it as the Feinstein house. He trudged up the few steps to the front door and rang.

The little gook answered the bell.

"Is the master home?" asked Wyatt.

"Yes," said Chiun, Master of Sinanju, holder of the extreme mysteries of the martial arts, assassin whose labors supported the village of Sinanju in Korea, as his father's labor had supported the village, as his father's father's labors had supported the village, all by renting themselves to those with the money to pay for their services.

"May I speak with him?"

"You are," said Chiun.

"I mean Mr. Blomberg."

Sheriff Wyatt watched. The little gook smiled an amused little smile and bowed. Frail little fellow, thought Wyatt. Funny, he did not invite the sheriff in, so as the little gook began to shuffle off to get his queerio boss, Wyatt stepped into the house behind him.

And suddenly, surprisingly, there was a sharp pain in the sheriff's gut and a blur as if the little old man's hand had come out from behind him with a knife in it, and Sheriff Wyatt heard:

"You were not invited in."

And the little gook hadn't even broken his shuffling stride, and he had left a knife in Wyatt's stomach. Wyatt just knew it, and he was afraid to look. He clutched the searing pain, feeling for the blood he knew must be there.

"Oh, sweet mercy, Jesus, no," moaned Sheriff Wyatt. He felt gingerly around the deep wound. No blood yet. His hand could go no farther. He steadied himself against the frame of the door. He groaned, praying that the other white man would find him. Then he heard a voice that had to be Remo Blomberg's.

"Chiun, c'mon, will you please?"

Then the gook's voice. "It is a nothing."

"Well, the sheriff doesn't think so."

"If I had killed him, you would have been upset. But do I get thanks for my thinking of your welfare? No. I get rebuke."

What the hell were they talking about? thought Sheriff Wyatt. It must be a knife that the sneaky little dink had slipped into him.

"Just lean back," said the white man. "Take your hands away from your stomach. That's it. Now keep your eyes shut just the way they are."

Sheriff Wyatt felt an even sharper pain around the wound like a hand slapping, opening the knife wound farther, and then he felt no pain at all. The no pain felt so good that tears welled in his eyes before he knew they were there.

He opened his eyes and looked down for the knife the white man must have removed. But there was no knife. There was no wound. There was no mark on his shirt. A miracle. He always knew Jews knew the mysteries of miracle healing.

"Thank you, thank you," said the sheriff, regaining his composure. "What did you do with the knife?"

"What knife?"

"The one the little gook stuck in me."

"There was no knife."

"I know a knife wound when I been wounded. I'm charging that little dink with assaulting an officer with a deadly weapon."

"Do you have any pain?"

"No."

"Do you have a wound?"

"Doesn't look like it."

"Then how are you going to accuse him of sticking a knife in you?"

"There are ways we have," said Sheriff Wyatt, hitching up his gunbelt.

"Look. He never cut you. He just affected nerves beneath the skin. Painful. But harmless."

"Oh," said Sheriff Wyatt, peering past Remo Blomberg at the frail creature standing calmly and quietly in repose near a vase, as if both were moulded from the same frail piece of porcelain. "Listen boy," Wyatt boomed to the elderly Oriental. "Next time you try any of that funny business with stomach nerves and stuff, you had it, boy. Heah? Don't say I didn't warn you."

There it was. Those grins. Those queerio grins on both this Remo Blomberg fella and that gook. Like the grins the day before, when they arrived, and they glanced at the notches on his gun and just smiled goose-faced at each other like two fagolas.

"That goes for you too, Mr. Blomberg, no disrespect meant, but where would any of you be without the law?"

"Call me Remo," said the young new owner of Feinstein's.

"Sure, Remo," said Sheriff Wyatt.

In the car Wyatt said he was not familiar with Jewish names and what did Remo stand for?

"It's not really a Jewish name," said Remo.

"Yeah, what kind is it then?"

"It's a long story," said Remo. He wore a white sports shirt and blue slacks with Italian slip-on shoes. He felt very relaxed.

"We got time," said Sheriff Wyatt.

"It's a long story I'm not going to tell you," Remo said. Then he smiled.

"Well, sure. If it's personal and all. You'll find out, though, that out here in San Aquino everybody sort of gets to know everybody else's stories. Know what I mean?"

"No," said Remo. And they drove in silence to the Curpwell Building where the night watchman let them in. They went past the rows of desks on the first floor, into a secretary's office that was open, then Wyatt stopped, knocked at the polished thick wooden door with its brass inlays.

It opened and Lester Curpwell IV, in dark business suit with vest and a brave smile warming out of a concerned face, greeted Remo with a big handshake.

"I'm glad to meet you but sorry to meet you under these circumstances," he said.

Remo looked puzzled, although he wasn't. He accepted Curpwell's hand and noticed Wyatt look with contempt at the limp wrist.

70

"Yes, it's confusing," Curpwell conceded. "I'll explain everything, Mr. Blomberg," he said.

Remo noticed two middle-aged men, one dressed casually and the other more formally, standing at seats around a long, dark conference table with a warm yellow overhead light that made the meeting look like a conspiracy. He knew what would be happening, but he must act surprised, he reminded himself.

"Call me Remo," said Remo.

Curpwell graciously led him to the table and introduced him to a Dourn Rucker—call him Dourn—and a Mitchell Boydenhousen—call him Sonny. He watched their eyes as he offered a limp hand, then another limp hand. They hid their embarrassment with dishonest warmth.

Remo could see Wyatt was giving the ceiling an "oh, no, not another bleeding heart" look. Fine.

Remo eased himself into one of the tan leather chairs surrounding the table. The room tasted and smelled of good wood, fine polish and top grade leather, all put together over a century. People sometimes tried to provide this solid conservative feel in a day and discovered they could not get it. They could buy the tables, the lamps and the leather. Even the fireplace and the portrait behind the desk at the end of the room. But they found they lacked the taste of generations of accepted wealth.

Remo crossed a leg, a bit more gracefully than was necessary. Chiun often warned him against overacting. Chiun, in situations like these, was very much the method school of acting. To play the innocent flower, be the innocent flower. Your claws can always surface.

Remo tried to set the men, something Chiun had been working on him for years. That extra sense of danger, who was a killer and who was not. Chiun sometimes could chart the violence in a man's heart and compute exactly how much would be used.

One night in a restaurant in Kansas City, Chiun had Remo scan the crowd and pick out those who were dangerous. Remo picked three men and couldn't narrow it down any further. Before the night ended, an old woman in a flowered hat tried to kill Remo with a hat pin. The men were harmless.

Chiun had known it was her by instinct.

Now Remo tried. He sat around the table with the four men and he graded them and this time he was sure he was right.

Wyatt might kill somebody by accident. The notches in the gun were for what he thought he should be, not what he was.

Rucker and Boydenhousen appeared like fairly healthy specimens and might, if circumstances led them to it, or if backed into it, kill.

But Lester Curpwell IV, with the fine, graying temples, the honest blue eyes and the strong but warm sympathetic smile of America's nobility. ... He could drive a spike through your retina and not miss a meal.

"We face a serious problem here in San Aquino, Mr. Blomberg," said Curpwell, folding his strong hands together as in prayer. "This is earthquake country, you know."

"That wasn't explained to me when I bought Feinstein's."

"I guess everyone thought everyone else knew. By and large, earthquakes are like any other natural disasters. Things you risk, like getting hit by lightning. A man could, as they say, get killed walking across the street."

"Yes. But in an earthquake, the street walks across

you," Remo responded. "And if you have a store, it tears it down."

Remo saw Boydenhousen exchange glances with Rucker, and Sheriff Wyatt extend his manliness to a smothered snort.

"Well, that may be, but earthquakes and tremors are a part of life in California. I believe we've had fewer people killed here by quakes than by car accidents."

"We've had fewer people killed in Vietnam than in car accidents," Remo said.

Remo drummed his fingers. He caught hostility from Wyatt and confusion from Boydenhousen and Rucker. From Curpwell, he got the continued, unruffled presentation. Curpwell was a killer. The earthquakes were his show. No doubt about it.

"Since you feel that way," Curpwell said, "it makes this meeting easier. We are in a position to guarantee you no more earthquake worries."

"Put it in a bottle," Remo said. "I'll drink it."

Curpwell went on to tell the story: how Sheriff Wyatt had been contacted by people who could sell earthquake insurance. Not payment after damages were incurred by earthquakes, but prevention. And after a demonstration, the leaders of San Aquino had decided to pay. Eight thousand dollars a month, twelve months a year.

"Who are these people who sell the insurance?" Remo asked.

"We don't know," said Lester Curpwell IV. "Sheriff Wyatt delivers the money, but he's never seen them."

"You pay a small fortune to someone for protection and you don't know to whom you're paying it? Is that what I'm being asked to believe?"

"I never see them," insisted Sheriff Wyatt, leaning

forward under the yellow light so that his reddish face oranged in its glow.

"What do you mean, you never see them?," Remo said. "They're ghosts? They're little elves? What?"

Wyatt was getting huffy. "I never saw them. They called on the phone. They told me where to leave the money. I left it. That's all," he said heatedly.

"You talk to them on the phone," Remo said. "So they have voices. What are they? Squeaky little Munchkins? Moog synthesizers? Men? Women? What kind of sheriff are you, anyway?"

Wyatt half rose to his feet. "They're men," he roared, "and I hope you have a chance to meet them sometime!"

"This isn't really advancing our discussion," Curpwell interrupted. He explained how the four wealthiest men in San Aquino had to pay the tab. To prevent panic. To keep the area growing. To make the small investment against earthquakes to protect their big investment in the area's growth. All in secret. The quake people demanded secrecy.

"And who decided who would pay?," Remo asked.

"Well, I guess I did," said Lester Curpwell.

"And you own the big banking investment place here, right?"

"Right."

"So you would naturally know who had the money, right?"

"Right."

"And now, because I own Feinstein's, you assume I'm going to fork over $24,000 a year to you," said Remo. When he said "you," he looked directly at Curpwell.

"Not exactly," said Curpwell, looking down at his hands. "You see, because of the Feinstein incident—

he had disobeyed instructions and reported the whole thing to Washington—we had a quake last night."

"I didn't feel anything," Remo said.

"Well, it was a low one on the Mercalli intensity scale and only inferior structures were damaged. Your home is not an inferior structure."

"Just some wetbacks got killed. No one hurt," contributed Sheriff Wyatt. Curpwell looked pained.

He said, "Sheriff Wyatt got a phone call that the quake was in retribution for Feinstein's contacting Washington. And now the tab has been raised. It's $4,000 a month for each of us. Look at it this way, Mr. Blomberg. It's an investment. A good investment."

"If it's such a good investment, keep it to yourself."

"Look, Remo," said Dourn Rucker. "It's for all our benefits."

"Fine. Enjoy it. I don't intend to pay for it."

Rucker brought a fist down on the heavy table. Remo looked at Rucker disdainfully and dandled a foot.

"I can't afford to pay a third of $16,000 a month," Rucker growled. "I don't have that much. I have trouble paying $2,000 a month."

Remo contained a smile. It was working. He might even have the whole thing wrapped up in a day or two. In a voice of angel's clarion innocence, Remo asked:

"Why bother to pay at all?"

"Because I want my family in one piece and my business in one piece. These people have us by the balls. By the balls, Feinstein."

"Blomberg," Remo corrected.

"By the balls, Blomberg."

"Then," said Remo, "why not let Curpwell here pay? I mean, he's the wealthiest man here. He practically owns the valley. The welcome wagon brochure says they almost named the town Curpwell, except the monks got here first."

"That's correct," Curpwell said, and Remo saw his back stiffen.

"So why don't you pay it?"

"I don't think it's fair that one man should pay."

"Then why should four pay? Why don't you collect the whole thing in taxes?"

" 'Cause it has to be secret," interrupted Wyatt.

"Why? Is it some kind of fraternity? A masonic lodge?," asked Remo.

" 'Cause the insurance people want it that way, that's why," said Wyatt haughtily. "You ain't even in this town one day and you're telling us how to survive. That's brass. That's real brass. Only one kind of people have that kind of brass."

"Please," said Curpwell to Sheriff Wyatt, and to Remo: "We've been warned to let no one in authority know. Feinstein talked and last night seven died in an earthquake, Mr. Blomberg."

"Call me Remo."

"Mr. Blomberg," repeated Curpwell. "Feinstein, Harris Feinstein did not die of food poisoning. He was murdered. He told authorities in Washington and he was murdered. Along with a man from the Interior Department."

Remo smiled. "Beautiful," he said. He saw Rucker's eyebrows raise. Boydenhousen leaned forward. Only Sheriff Wyatt seemed oblivious to what was going on. Curpwell's eyes became cold.

"Beautiful," Remo repeated. Then he turned to Rucker and Boydenhousen. "Are you people really paying or are you with Curpwell?"

Rucker blinked. Boydenhousen said: "I don't understand."

"Are you guys paying?"

"Yes," said Rucker. Boydenhousen nodded.

"All right," said Remo. "I'm going to save you some money right now. Don't pay. There's your earthquake insurance man. More like a blackmailer, I'd say." He pointed a limp-wristed upward-curving finger at the mouth of Lester Curpwell IV. The pinky played at the verge of a digression. Remo went on:

"He's the man who chose you. He's the man who threatened me with death. I mean, if you listened to him as I did, he was telling me just now I'd get killed like Feinstein if I didn't pay up."

Rucker and Boydenhousen looked at each other.

"No," they said in unison. "We don't believe you."

But Remo smiled to himself, because he had won. So much for the next payment. Now it was up to the earthquake people to move. And when they did, Remo would offer their remnants to the seven who had died the night before, but especially to a baby, who, someone had told him, cried all night.

# CHAPTER ELEVEN

It was not a hard decision. One did not have to register it on a seismograph or run it through one of the large computers at Richter Institute.

Remo whatever-his-name-was had to die. It had to be done. Why did Sheriff Wade Wyatt find this so objectionable? The young bubbling female voices waited for an answer.

Wade Wyatt sat on a hard wooden chair and looked out the trailer window at the late summer moon. He didn't like to look at *them*.

He changed the subject. "You were with Feinstein, weren't you?" he said. "He wasn't queer or anything. You killed him, right?"

"Yes," came the sweet, gentle voice. The other voice added, "and the government man too."

"I thought that they was both queers."

"You would, pig."

"Hey, now," Wyatt protested.

"Hey, now, shut up, pig, or you'll go the same way. And you'll go the same way if you don't take care of this Remo. We're not going to let anybody stop us."

"I can't do that," Wyatt said. "I can't kill him."

"But you will. You will, just like you phoned Washington to report Feinstein. You will, just like you've collected the money for us. You'll do it, because you're afraid not to. We can't have somebody screwing up this whole thing."

"I don't want to."

"Dammit. You've got notches on your gun, pig. Live up to them."

"I can't. I can't."

"But you will."

Wade Wyatt closed his eyes. He waited. Then he opened his eyes. He turned his head. They were gone. They weren't going to kill him.

He got up and left the trailer quickly. He'd call it a standoff. He never agreed to kill that Remo Blomberg. So they couldn't say he backed off.

But they were tough for broads. When push came to shove, they'd do Remo Blomberg. And he did not let his mind dwell on what fagola queerio Blomberg would look like when they were done with him.

Man, what tough broads.

# CHAPTER TWELVE

It was two days after the earthquake that killed seven Mexicans that Don Fiavorante Pubescio, sunning his large body by his very blue and very big swimming pool, heard something very interesting from a paisan.

The man was a grape grower. He lived in San Aquino. The man's father was a friend of Pubescio's father. Yes, Don Fiavorante knew of the man's father very well.

Don Fiavorante courteously extended a seat to his guest and just as courteously accepted the man's kiss on his hand.

"We are friends," said Don Fiavorante. "My father was your father's friend. Our friendship precedes the womb, Robert Gromucci. May I offer you a drink?"

Robert Gromucci, in a very light summer suit, nervously accepted the seat in a red-webbed chair by the pool.

"Do not believe all the bad things you hear about me, friend," said Don Fiavorante in a soft, gentle manner, almost pleading except that Don Fiavorante never pleaded. "There is no need to be nervous. Do you think I do not know that your workers are planning to leave? Do you think I do not know that this is your most important harvest? That if it fails, you fail? Do you think I forget where your first wine has gone every year? Do you think I forget you when I drink the wine? Do not be nervous, my friend."

Robert Gromucci grinned. Like a little boy, he grinned; like a little boy whose father has told him everything will be all right.

The noon-baked pool smelled of chlorine but Robert Gromucci did not smell it. Nor did he notice the butler bringing a fresh lemon drink, dripping beads of cold moisture on the frosted glass.

Robert Gromucci talked and noticed nothing, because at last he was with someone who understood him. He talked about his money needs and his labor problems. He told about the earthquake—how he and his wife did not even notice the tremors. He told about the grape pickers. He told about the sheriff and about Sonny Boydenhousen, who handled insurance as well as real estate and with whom Gromucci had talked that morning. Boydenhousen, an old boyhood chum, had looked shocked and so Robert Gromucci asked. He wanted to know why. But Sonny Boydenhousen didn't want to say. He did not want Robert Gromucci to lose faith in Les Curpwell.

"Les Curpwell?," Gromucci had asked, stunned.

"Yes. Les Curpwell." Les Curpwell was behind the earthquakes but Sonny was only telling Robert because it had come as such a shock.

Robert Gromucci was so relieved, sitting by the swimming pool, knowing he had a protector, that he did not mind answering all the sudden questions from Don Fiavorante Pubescio.

Who? How much? How often? How? You don't know how? They will pay? They won't pay? Only San Aquino pays? None of the other towns? You don't know how much?

Les Curpwell, you say?

"Yes," said Don Fiavorante Pubescio, the hot California sun baking his browning body. "A fine man, Mr. Curpwell. I have heard of him. One can reason with him, I hear. He knows how to make an earthquake, you say?"

Don Fiavorante said he wished only small interest on the loan. Twenty per cent a year. To run, you know, what is the word, I am so foolish with words, yes, thank you, compounded monthly.

And later, Don Fiavorante noted that it sounded impossible about the earthquake business and Robert Gromucci should not worry the more about it.

"Earthquakes come from Blessed God," said Don Fiavorante, who ordered himself a cup of tea, because his doctor had ordered him to drink only tea, and also ordered a checkbook. "You don't want to carry $55,-000 in cash with you, do you, Robert, my friend?"

"What good will the money do?" Gromucci asked. "I need workers."

"Extra money for extra workers. A bonus here, a bonus there."

"But my workers say the earthquake was only the beginning. They say gods from mountains will meet gods from valleys. They say my ranch is cursed and they will not work there."

"Yes. Well, we do this little thing two ways. You give your pickers a slight raise. You keep much of this money in reserve. I want you to have leeway. I have men who work for me and they will speak to your workers. They will explain to them that earthquakes are a less definite threat to their lives than other things."

Robert Gromucci hated to disagree with Don Fiavorante. "They will run. They will run. There are two men in town now, who bring strangeness. New men and my pickers are afraid of them."

83

"They threaten your pickers?" asked Don Fiavorante.

"No. They keep to themselves."

"They why are they a threat?"

"My pickers are superstitious. They are still pagans, these Mexicans. They are afraid of these two men, because they fear these two men bring death."

"Then we handle this three ways. I will send some people to reason with these two men and explain to them how they can help you. We will explain it to them so carefully that they cannot refuse. What are their names?"

"The younger man just bought Feinstein's Department Store. His name is Blomberg. Remo Blomberg. The other man is Oriental. Very old and feeble. His name is Chiun."

Don Fiavorante got their address, assured his friend that all would be well, got his tea and his checkbook from his butler, then wrote out the check to Gromucci, who kissed his hand and was gone.

Then Don Fiavorante got down to serious business. He called a council of his capos. Not for the morrow, not for the evening, but for now. His requests were politely voiced, but there was nothing polite about them. A stranger might even assume that he was begging. But for a beggar, he was very successful. Men interrupted meals, business conferences, naps, even lovemaking—when Don Fiavorante Pubescio asked politely to see them immediately. Not a few made a quick stop at a church on the way to light a candle. But no one refused to come.

They met in Don Fiavorante's study. They kissed his hand when they entered and he greeted them all warmly, like a father seeing his sons after long vacations. The Cadillacs stretched the length of his driveway and out into the street, but Don Fiavorante did not mind. It would be a brief meeting, and the Bel Condor police would delay traffic through the block— all traffic that was not expressly invited into Don Fiavorante's block.

When all seventeen men were seated, Don Fiavorante began. Within three seconds, he displayed more intelligence and insight than the United States State Department.

"Let us get to business," he said. A terry cloth robe draped his rolling belly. His face was strangely soft. Yet the words he spoke were listened to with respect by the men, some of whose faces would freeze an Olympic flame and the crowd along with it.

"For a short while," Don Fiavorante began, "I have suspected something. It was just a suspicion, a little thing that one plays in one's mind and takes no heed because it seems unusual. That suspicion was confirmed today. We can be more successful, more powerful than at anytime in our lives. We can win respect for us as we have never truly had respect for us. And in places where we never had respect before."

He paused, looking at the faces he knew, looking at the minds he knew, the habits he knew, the actions he knew, wondering at this moment standing in his den if these men were ready for the greatness now to be thrust upon them.

"Heroin," said Don Fiavorante, "is chickenfeed. Numbers, chickenfeed. Horses, chickenfeed. Stolen autos, chickenfeed. Prostitution, chickenfeed. Chickenfeed."

Don Fiavorante watched the men hide their disbelief. For any other man to have said what he said would have met with scorn. For Don Fiavorante, it was polite concern on interested faces.

85

He would push them one step further, because they must understand.

"And yet, for all this venture holds in store for us, it also holds terror beyond anything we have ever known."

"Not the atomic bomb?" said Gummo the Pipe Barussio.

There was silence again, indicating that if Don Fiavorante told all assembled that he had an atomic bomb, well, why shouldn't he have? Who better to trust with one?

But Don Fiavorante said: "Not an atomic bomb, my good friend, Gummo. An atomic bomb is chicken-feed." And on that note, with some eyebrows raised, a few mouths open and all reserve gone, Don Fiavorante told the assembly about his plan, a modern version of the shakedown. And he told them about a quirk of nature called the San Andreas Fault. Only this time, it wasn't just a few lives and windows and a small town in a small county that was threatened.

It was an entire state.

And it wasn't just a handful of rich businessmen who would be asked to pay. It would be the richest of the rich of the world. The United States Government.

"Why not? They got the money," pointed out Don Fiavorante reasonably. "If they spend thirty billion dollars a year on Vietnam, what do you think they'll pay for California?"

"Too big, too big," said Gummo the Pipe Barussio. He pointed out it was too easy to get crushed by something like the United States government.

Don Fiavorante smiled.

"We don't really have a choice. We either hold the weapon or have it held at us. It exists. There are people who can make mountains move and valleys jump."

And then Don Fiavorante began answering questions, explaining about California and what he knew.

"What is this thing that makes the earth buckle?" asked Manny the Pick Musso.

Don Fiavorante did not know yet.

"Can we turn earthquakes on and off like a faucet?"

Don Fiavorante did not know yet.

"More powerful than an atomic bomb?" asked Gummo the Pipe Barussio again.

When the United States bombed Hiroshima, it was rebuilt. When earthquakes claim a city, it disappears. The famous city of Troy for example. Never to come again. Thus spoke Don Fiavorante Pubescio.

"How much money?" asked Musso, who loved money even more than he loved women and for that reason was trusted by Don Fiavorante.

How much money could Musso spend in a hundred lifetimes? Don Fiavorante's question ended the questioning.

It would be simple, Don Fiavorante said. Musso would take several men and go see Lester Curpwell. They would make him talk. From him, they would learn the secret of the earthquake power. They would reason with him. Reason thoroughly with him until he told everything. Lester Curpwell IV needed money. Don Fiavorante knew that. The Curpwell holdings were in trouble. If Lester Curpwell IV wanted money, Manny the Pick Musso was to give him money. Whatever he wanted. Whatever it took for him to talk.

Musso's lined tan face was as calm as wax.

"How much?," he asked.

"A million dollars, if he wants it. They're amateurs running this shakedown," said Don Fiavorante.

"Amateurs. Pros are going to move in now. And a million for the secret is chickenfeed."

"And suppose I can get it without money?" Musso asked.

"Fine. But get everything he knows. I don't want excuses. I want the way he does it and if you do not get so simple a thing, I might have cause to believe that you are holding out on me."

The wax face did not move. Only the palms of Manny the Pick Musso became damp. Musso would get the information from Curpwell or spend the rest of his life running from Don Fiavorante's men.

It was not lost on him that his personal situation was comparable to that which Don Fiavorante said faced the entire organization. Be conquerors or victims. But wasn't that the lesson of life, the lesson of Sicily?

To Gummo the Pipe Barussio, Don Fiavorante gave the problem of the Gromucci vineyards. Don Fiavorante was sure it could be solved by putting some men on the Gromucci ranch to work on the pickers a little bit.

Gummo the Pipe Barussio lowered his head. He whispered in an even lower voice than normal. He whispered so that his own consigliore sitting in the back of the room would not hear.

"Don Fiavorante, I have worked well with you, yes?"

"Yes, Gummo, my friend. You have.

"I have never before refused an offer of good work?"

"You have not."

"Don Fiavorante, I ask then a favor. I have premonitions. Fears. Dreams. I seek less danger this time. Is there something less that I can do?"

Don Fiavorante nodded.

"As you will. Less danger is less rewards, although convincing wetbacks to work is not exactly armed robbery. Still, you have a right to ask. There is another way to do it. In San Aquino, there are two newcomers. The grape pickers are frightened of these men. Superstition. Go to see the men. Tell them to talk to the workers at the Gromucci farm and tell them that there is no superstition that the workers need fear. Let the workers see these two men. Let them see that the two men are afraid of you. Then, when that is done, I think there will be no more trouble at the Gromucci farms."

Gummo the Pipe Barussio smiled. He kissed Don Fiavorante's hand lavishly.

"This may seem like a flippancy, Don Fiavorante, but I have a premonition of a swift death. And I believe it. Thank you. I had dreams of hands moving faster than arrows in the air. Faster than that. Thank you."

"Each man's foolishness on the outside is his real truth on the inside," said Don Fiavorante. And before he discharged Gummo the Pipe Barussio, he gave him the names of the two men he must talk to.

One was an ancient, dying Oriental. His name was Chiun.

The other was a department store owner. If the stories could be believed, a—how-you-say?—fairy.

His name was Remo.

# CHAPTER THIRTEEN

The custom-built Cadillac convertible spewed gravel as it rolled up the winding driveway to the home of Remo Blomberg, department store entrepreneur.

The car's white nylon top was up, warding off the California sun. The air conditioning was on full blast, chilling the left knee of Freddy Palermo, the driver, and the right knee of Marty Albanese, the front seat passenger.

Nevertheless, Gummo the Pipe Barussio, sitting alone on the soft glove leather of the back seat, was sweating. He was a big man and wrinkled, but his wrinkles had the character of prunes and his bigness was not the fat of pork. His hair was cut close to his head and even though he was in his early fifties, there was not a single gray strand. His hair was still shiny and blue-black and his skin was tanned, the olive-tan of Mediterranean people who know how to tan without drying out.

But still he sweated. He wiped his forehead carefully with an expensive white linen handkerchief which had been pressed into knife-sharp edges when they had left, but which was now sodden and damp with the sweat of one hundred nervous miles.

He was pretty sure now that he had made a mistake in bringing along Freddy Palermo and Marty Albanese. Sure, they were street tough, but they were young, inclined to be flip and to look for trouble when trouble was not really inevitable. They would have been fine in the old days in Chicago. But this wasn't Chicago and today the Mafia flourished by avoiding trouble.

But could you tell that to these punks? Could you tell them that it was better to convince someone with talk than with muscle—even though Gummo the Pipe Barussio was not afraid to use muscle? His nickname did not refer to his smoking habits.

You could try to tell them that, but they didn't listen. None of the old ways, the old beliefs, was good enough for them. He had made the mistake on the drive over of telling them about his premonition of hands moving faster than arrows and they had both chuckled. Someday they might learn, but for today they were the wrong men.

Yet they were still the sons of his two sisters, and family meant something when you picked the people for the good jobs—the big, important jobs.

Barussio was grateful that Don Fiavorante had seen fit to change his assignment. That premonition had been very real. But even with his new assignment— the old Oriental and the fairy department store owner—he felt a vague unease. He would be very happy to be back home at poolside.

"Listen," he said, leaning forward over the soft red leather of the front seat. "Keep your mouths closed. No wiseass stuff. I'll do the talking."

"Okay, Uncle Gummo," said Palermo. Albanese just grunted.

The car rolled to a stop in front of the large double doors that were the front entrance to the Blomberg home.

Albanese opened the passenger's door and quickly

slid out. He did not hold the door for Barussio. The door slipped back, and Barussio stopped it with his foot, pushing it open again to get out. Yes, Albanese was a mistake. Not only hot-tempered, but no manners, no discipline. As he got out, Barussio hissed to Palermo: "Keep an eye on Marty, so he don't cause no trouble."

"Gotcha," Palermo said.

Palermo got out on his side of the car and joined Barussio in the walk to the front door. Albanese had already jabbed the bell nervously and Barussio elbowed him away from the front of the door.

Gummo the Pipe rang the bell again. He heard it tingle inside. He listened closely but heard no footsteps. Then, noiselessly, the door swung open and he was faced by an aged Oriental, wearing a long, blue, brocaded robe.

The Pipe suppressed a smile of relief. He was glad he had asked not to have to hassle the wet backs. This way would be easier. This old man? Why, he was easily eighty years old and could be no more than five feet tall. He would never see one hundred pounds again.

His nails were long and pointy. Little tufts of hair on top of his head and stringing from his chin made him look like the owner of a curio shop in a cheap movie.

"Did you come on the sightseeing bus? Is that why you gawk?" the old man said.

"I'm sorry," Barussio said quickly. "I was expecting someone else."

"I am no one else; I am only me."

Albanese snickered loudly and Barussio glared at him before speaking again.

"Is your name Chan?"

"My name is Chiun. Chan is a Chinese name." The

old man spit into the gravel alongside the front porch, barely missing the toe of Albanese's right shoe. Barussio blinked in surprise.

"I have business to discuss with you. May we come in? It's hot out here," Barussio asked.

"You are the leader of this group?"

"Yes."

"Then you may come in. Your servants may wait outside. Particularly the ugly, impolite one." He bowed to Albanese.

"Certainly," Barussio said and stepped through the door.

Albanese's eyes narrowed. Well, Marty Albanese didn't have to put up with that. Being called a servant by a dink. Ugly and impolite too. And that old has-been uncle, Barussio, agreeing. Why didn't he speak up? Albanese was definitely unhappy. He stepped toward the door to enter behind Barussio. Then his stomach suddenly hurt and he clutched it as the old dink shut the door behind Barussio.

"Wotsa matter?," Palermo asked.

"Don't know. Little cramp or something," he said, clutching his stomach. "It's all right now. Snotty little gook. Be a pleasure to take some of the starch out of him."

Inside, Barussio was escorted into a cool living room and motioned to a seat on a blue suede sofa.

He sat and Chiun stood facing him. Their eyes were still almost level.

"Now, your business."

"I don't quite know how to say this," Barussio began.

"Try saying whatever comes to your mind."

"Well, Mr. Chiun, a friend of mine is having trouble at his grape farm and it appears you are the cause of it."

"I?"

"Yes. The workers, you see, are very superstitious. There was a minor earthquake the other night, and now they are refusing to work because you have come to town. They say you bring some kind of Oriental curse, if you'll pardon the expression." Barussio had stopped sweating. He was relaxed now and he leaned back casually against the soft suede cushions.

Chiun only nodded, but said nothing.

Barussio waited for a comment, but when none came, he said; "They also feel that your employer ... is his name Remo?"

"Yes, Remo," Chiun interjected.

"Yes. Well, the workers feel he too has some kind of power and they refuse to work."

"And so?" Chiun asked.

Dammit, he was exasperating. He gave nothing.

"So we would like you and Mr. Remo to accompany us to the grape farm and to tell the workers that there is nothing special about you. Just let them see you, so that they know you're not some kind of ghosts or something."

Chiun nodded and folded his hands under the broad flowing sleeves of his robe. He walked to the front window and looked out at where Palermo and Albanese leaned on the front fender of the Cadillac.

"That is all?" Chiun said.

"Yes," Barussio said, and he chuckled. "It's really kind of a silly thing and you and Mr. Remo would have a perfect right to think it was stupid, but it's very important to my friend because it's harvesting time and if his workers don't work, his vineyards will be ruined. Just a drive of a few minutes." Yes, he was glad he didn't go the other route; that he had convinced Don Fiavorante of the sense of doing this without violence and threats.

"Will you do it?"

"I will," said Chiun. "But I don't know if Mr. Blomberg will."

"Is he here? May I ask him?"

"He is here. I shall ask him. Please wait here."

Chiun turned and shuffled away, his hands still hidden inside his sleeves, his feet noiseless, even on the stone floor. He walked slowly up the two small stairs to the dining room, and then slid open a floor-to-ceiling glass door and stepped out into a suddenly-sunny yard.

Barussio watched him walk away. The hot wedge of air that had slipped through the glass door before Chiun closed it now marched across the dining room, into the living room, and hit Barussio in the face. He did not even reach for his handkerchief; he had nothing to sweat about anymore.

Chiun walked across the gray flagstone and slate patio to the large kidney-shaped swimming pool. He stood on the edge of the pool and looked down accusingly, like a meticulous housewife trying to stare away an unexpected spot.

The crystal waters of the pool were motionless. Through them, at the bottom of the pool, eight feet below his feet, Chiun could see Remo, wearing bathing trunks, lying on his back, his hands grasping the lowest metal step. He saw Chiun and waved.

Chiun crooked an imperious finger toward him and motioned for him to surface.

Remo waved at Chiun to go away.

Chiun again summoned Remo with his index finger.

Remo rolled over on the bottom of the pool, his feet fluttering just enough to keep him down, and he turned face down so he could not see Chiun.

Chiun looked around him on the patio. On a poolside table he spotted a giant chromium machine-nut, used as a decorative ashtray, and picked it up. Carefully, he extended the heavy nut over the pool ladder, then dropped it. It hit the water with a splash, then sloshed down, and hit the back of Remo's head.

Remo spun around, saw the gadget, picked it up and shot to the top of the pool.

He was shouting as soon as he broke through the surface of the water.

"Dammit, Chiun, that hurt."

"You are like the proverbial jackass. You perform well, but first it is necessary to get your attention."

Remo hung off the ladder with his right hand and looked at the watch on his left wrist.

"You really screwed me up," he said. "Five minutes and twenty seconds. This was the day I was going to make six minutes."

"If I had known that Dr. Smith sent you here to practice for the Olympics, I would not have disturbed you. But because I thought you had something else in mind, I thought it worthwhile telling you that we have visitors."

Remo pulled himself up to the flagstones. "Visitors?" he said. He dropped the metal nut to the stone deck where it hit with a sharp clack.

"Yes," Chiun said, "visitors. I think they represent your country's criminal element."

"What do they want with us?"

"They want us to go convince Mexicans to pick grapes."

"Why us? I ain't Cesar Chavez."

"Apparently the earthquake and our arrival in this community have caused some fears among these Mexicans. They think we are some kind of gods."

"What do you think?"

97

"I think we should go," Chiun said, "and tell them the truth."

"Which is?"

"Which is that I am but a frail old Oriental servant and you are a champion swimmer in training. And we should see what else these criminals may want from us."

"As you wish, little father," Remo said, bowing from the waist.

"Get your clothes on, honorable son," Chiun said.

Chiun went back through the glass door into the dining room, while Remo went through another set of glass doors into his bedroom to dry and dress.

Barussio looked up as Chiun approached.

"He agrees," Chiun said.

Barussio was relieved. "My friend will be very happy," he said. "It is important to him."

Chiun was silent.

After two minutes, Remo came padding quietly into the living room. He wore white leather tennis shoes with no socks, white slacks and a white knitted short-sleeved shirt.

"Hello, I'm Blomberg," he said, extending a firm hand to Barussio, before remembering that it should have been limp.

Barussio stood up. "Has your man explained things to you?" He didn't really look like a fairy, Barussio thought. Good handshake too. Still, you never could tell. Particularly in California. Suntans can hide anything, he thought.

"Yeah," Remo said. "He explained. It didn't make much sense, but it's a nice day to take somebody for a ride."

Barussio's ears picked up at the phrase but Remo Blomberg was still smiling insipidly. He meant nothing by it.

Chiun led the way out the front door and Palermo and Albanese stood up next to the car when they saw the three men coming. Albanese saw Remo come out last and put his hand to his mouth. "Look at Doctor Kildare," he said in a stage whisper, meant to be loud enough for Remo to hear.

Barussio glared. Chiun looked on with equanimity. Remo walked up to Albanese and said, "Hiya, fella. How's tricks?"

"Oh, tricks are just fine," Albanese said. "Just fine."

With a mock curtsey, he opened the Cadillac door and waved the three men in. Chiun got in first, then Remo and as Barussio stepped by Albanese, he hissed: "Any more shit, I'm gonna pull your eyeballs out and squash 'em against a wall like grapes."

Albanese's face dropped. He'd have to watch his step. He got quietly into the car. Palermo got behind the wheel.

"Where to, Uncle Gummo?"

"To Bob Gromucci's farm," Gummo the Pipe Barussio said. The motor started and the air conditioning came on. It was not really necessary. Barussio was dry and cool. Why not? There was nothing to sweat about.

# CHAPTER FOURTEEN

But across town, in the office of the First Aquino Trust and Development Corporation, Lester Curpwell IV was sweating.

He faced two men. He had known they were trouble when they came in, without an announcement, without an appointment.

The tall man leading the way wore a dark blue suit that was hand-tailored. But even the tailor's art failed to conceal his muscular bulk. He almost rippled when he walked.

The man who followed him wore a brown suit with white shadow stripes. He had a face that was ratlike and twisted into a grim smile, as if he alone knew a joke that no one else had heard.

The burly man sat down in the chair facing Curpwell. The other man stood against the office door, his back to it, not too subtly shielding the office from intrusion. With a penknife, he began to clean his fingernails.

"Why don't you have a seat?" Curpwell said to the man facing him, who was already seated.

"No thanks. This one'll do fine," the man said.

"Well, now that you're in here, suppose you tell me what you want," Curpwell said.

"Sure. I'll make it simple, Curpwell. You're a businessman, right?"

"Yes, that's right."

"Well, I'm a businessman too. So no fancy-schmantz around the bush. I want to know your earthquake secret. I'll pay for it."

"Earthquake secret?" Curpwell said. His stomach turned over. Harris Feinstein was right. Curpwell should have gone with him to Washington. It was only a matter of time before the thing got out of hand. That's what Feinstein had said. He had been right. It was out of hand now.

"Yeah. Earthquake secret. I want to know how you do it so that you're able to shake down the people around here."

"I'm afraid, Mister. . . ." Curpwell waited for the man to fill in the blank but there was no response, so he went on: "that I don't know what you're talking about. I don't have any earthquake secrets. If you want to know about earthquakes, go see Doctor Quake at Richter Institute. Sign up for one of his seminars. But don't waste my time with nonsense."

"Curpwell, it can be easy or it can be hard. Have it your own way," Manny the Pick Musso said. "I want to know how you do it."

"And I don't know what you're talking about," Curpwell said, lowering his eyes to the desk where he had been reading a stack of financial reports showing that the Curpwell empire was in deep financial trouble. He did not look up, so he did not see the burly man in the blue suit nod to the man at the door. He did not see the coming of the blow against the back of his head.

And because he was unconscious, he did not see the big man in the blue suit slide a shiny icepick from his inside jacket pocket and carefully remove the cork from its gleaming dart-sharp point.

As he went into unconsciousness, Curpwell only

wished that he had made his report to the Presidential aide a little more danger-filled. Perhaps the government would not have just disregarded the whole thing. Perhaps they would have assigned someone to check it out. Someone who could have done something.

# CHAPTER FIFTEEN

The white Cadillac rolled between the banks of shade trees, along the red dusty road, kicking up sprays of grit that looked like powdered blood, which settled over and coated everything with the granular talcum of Southern California.

Off to the right, Remo could see a string of small tarpaper shacks—perhaps fifteen of them—and the rubble where other shacks once had stood. In front of the shacks, adults sat or stood and talked, and children ran in and out of their legs, playing with ropes, twigs and bits of ribbon.

The car screeched to a stop, rocking back and forth on over-soft springs. Albanese was out of the car before it stopped rocking.

The others stepped slowly from the cool, air-conditioned car into the heat of summer California. Albanese was already twenty-five feet away, talking to a wiry man with a drooping black mustache wearing dirty white pants and shirt of some rough, canvas-like material.

The pants and shirt were the right length but they drooped off the man as if they had once been tailored to fit, but—comfortably inside—the man had proceeded to lose thirty pounds.

The Mexican took off a natural colored straw hat and wiped his forehead with the back of his waist, as he listened to Albanese. Then he shrugged, a shrug that spoke of centuries of labor on someone else's land, turned and walked away toward the string of cabins, calling out names in Spanish as he went.

Albanese came back to meet Remo, Chiun and the two others as they slowly walked toward him, their toes kicking up small swirls of red powder.

"It's all right," he said, smiling. "That's Manuel. He's their leader. He's going to call the others. Then these two can talk to them."

"What should we say?" Remo asked.

Barussio said, "Just tell them that their fears of you are just a superstition. That there is nothing for them to worry about. Tell them it is okay for them to go back to work."

"Whatever you want," Remo said.

Chiun was craning his neck, inspecting the fields and hills of the grape farm.

Albanese stepped beside Remo. "Don't screw it up, sweetheart," he growled softly.

"Sweetheart? I didn't think you cared," Remo said.

"Just screw it up and you'll find out how much I care," Albanese said. "Might even have to get some dirt on your pretty little white suit."

"Oh, goodness gracious me!" Remo said.

A crowd was gathering now. Manuel had called the adults of the migrant camp and surrounded by children, they had begun to gather in a large clump. Manuel stepped to the forefront. "We are all here," he said.

Albanese nudged Remo in the ribs. "Talk to them," he said.

Remo stepped forward. "My name is Remo. This man is Chiun. What problems have we caused you?"

The adults looked around at each other, then at Manuel. They wore the same white uniforms Manuel did. Manuel said, "First there was the tearing of the earth and many of us died. Now the old folks tell us of more death to come. They say that death will surround us. And that death will come from you."

"Did they speak of us?" Remo asked.

"They spoke of an Oriental, an aged man of great wisdom. And they spoke of his white-faced companion whose hands are faster than sight and deadlier than arrows."

Albanese giggled. But Barussio heard. Hands that he could not see. He remembered his dream of hands, moving faster than sight, dealing out death. He felt a bead of perspiration form on his forehead.

"Who are these old folks of whom you speak?" Remo asked.

Manuel turned and spoke a few soft words in Spanish. The crowd parted. An old woman, as old as life and as weary as death, shuffled slowly through the crowd. She was dressed in black, and wore a black shawl. Her face was wrinkled and dry with the sorrow of centuries.

She stepped closely to Manuel's side. "I have seen the visions," she said to Remo. "I have seen the death of the fast hands coming."

"All right," Albanese growled to Remo. "Let's cut it short. Tell them to get back to work. Tell them to cut the shit and get back to work. If you and the gook know what's good for you, you'll move now."

Remo looked at Albanese next to him, registering his size and weight, then turned again to speak to Manuel. But Chiun had stepped forward, cool and imperturbable in his blue robes.

He walked up to the old woman and took her hands in his. They were the same size. Chiun and she stood there silently for a moment, their eyes locked together, neither speaking. Then Chiun stepped back.

107

His voice rang out across the field, echoing hollowly off the now-empty tarpaper shacks.

"Hear well my words," he said, intoning as if he were delivering a high mass.

"Your elders speak truth to you because there is death here. Your elders speak truth to you when they tell you of death to come, and your elders speak truth when they tell you of the man with the hands like arrows."

"What's he doing?" Albanese hissed. He and Palermo stepped forward behind Chiun, their towering presence meant to intimidate him.

"The men behind me are evil men," Chiun said, "and for such evil men, death is the only sure reward. It is the only fair compensation for their crimes."

Palermo and Albanese each grabbed one of Chiun's shoulders. Then they stopped grabbing and drew themselves up on tiptoes into erect positions, their faces contorted in pain, as Chiun dug his hands into their groins, without ever taking his eyes off the crowd of migrant workers.

"I say to you now that you should escape the death that will come. Listen to your elders. Return to your own land. They will tell you when the time has come that it is safe for you to return here, to return again to your work in the fields."

"Stop him," Barussio shouted to Palermo and Albanese.

Chiun's hands released their crushing hold on the two. They lunged at the frail yellow man in the blue kimono.

Palermo reached him first, then crumpled at Chiun's feet as if somehow his body had disappeared from inside his clothing and the empty garments just fell of their own weight.

"Gook bastard," Albanese cursed. "This is going to

be fun." He went at Chiun's throat with both hands to squeeze the life out of this old specter. His hands stopped working before they reached Chiun's throat. Then he was lifted off the ground, the force of an elbow crushing his windpipe, driving it upward into his mouth. His body followed, flying through the air, lifeless, to fall with a heavy thud at the feet of the woman in black. She looked down at Albanese's corpse, still writhing in death, and spit into his face.

She turned and the crowd split to make room for her. Without a word, she shuffled away, the adults behind her, herding their children along with whispers and pats on the backs of heads.

"Come back," Barussio shouted. "Come back. It's all a mistake."

"No mistake," Remo said.

Barussio reached into his jacket for his gun, a move he had not made in years but which he still did well.

The gun was out, in his hands, pointing at Chiun and his finger was squeezing the trigger. But his finger squeezed against only air as the gun dropped harmlessly to his feet.

Barussio began to turn toward Remo. In his dream, he had never seen the hand that killed him. He did not see it now. He did not even feel it. All he felt were the beads of perspiration on his head, his armpits suddenly clammy and wet, the sweat running in sudden spring rivulets down the insides of his thighs.

The perspiration was already beginning to show through his suit by the time his dead body reached the ground, kicking up the red dust into a small splash of dried blood.

Remo's eyes met Chiun's and the old man bowed. Remo returned the bow with mock courtesy.

Then he said, "Okay, Chiun, let's go. I've got some work to do."

As they walked slowly back toward the white Cadillac, leaving the three dead bodies on the ground behind them, Chiun said, "What is next?"

"I've had it. I'm going to go get the guy who sent these goons after us."

"Who might that be?" Chiun asked.

"Lester Curpwell IV," Remo said. "The guy behind all this."

# CHAPTER SIXTEEN

"Where's Curpwell, honeybunch?" asked Remo.

"He's inside his office," the young bronzed girl said. "But he sent out word not to disturb him for anything." She looked up and down Remo's body as if she regretted giving him that message.

"That's all right. He'll see me," Remo said, brushing past the girl's desk, walking toward the massive wood and brass doors to Curpwell's inner office.

"You can't go in there," the girl protested weakly. "He's already had two people barge in on him today. You can't go in there."

"Quiet, honey, or I'll shatter your charge card. I'm Remo Blomberg, the department store impresario."

The door was locked, the kind of lock in which a small pin shoots out from the lock mechanism and prevents the knob from turning. But if the knob is turned anyway, Remo found, the pin is sheared off and the door will open.

He pushed open the door. Curpwell was slumped forward on his desk. Remo covered the fifteen feet in just three steps.

Curpwell was not a pretty sight. His head lay on the desk blotter between his arms. His hands were threaded with small strings of blood from tiny puncture holes made in each finger and in the backs of his hands. There were the same puncture wounds in his ears and cheeks. Remo felt sticky blood under his fingers as he looked for a pulse in Curpwell's neck. There was only a faint pulsation.

Curpwell's secretary stood in the doorway, her hand to her mouth.

"Quick," Remo said. "Get a doctor. He's been hurt. Then call the sheriff. And for God's sake, close the door."

The doctor would do no good. He would be too late. The sheriff was as worthless as a banker's smile. But Remo did want the door closed. He wanted to be alone with the dying man.

He reached down inside Curpwell's shirt and with strong hands began to tap the chest in the area over the man's heart. He leaned Curpwell back into his chair and spoke into his ear.

"Curpwell, it's Remo. Remo Blomberg. What happened?"

Curpwell's eyes opened and Remo saw that they had been punctured too. Blood had dried inside each eye and they stared forward unseeing, each bearing a deep wound which had cost Curpwell his sight and would soon cost him his life.

"Curpwell. What happened?" Remo repeated.

"Remo." The man spoke slowly, agonizingly. "They thought I made earthquakes. Wanted me to tell secret."

"Who did?" Remo asked.

"Mafia. Man named Musso. Had an ice pick."

Remo's hands kept working on Curpwell's chest and the voice came a little stronger now.

"Remo? Remo Blomberg?"

"Yes. I'm right here."

"Mafia wants earthquake secret. You call . . . you call Captain Walters of State Police. Tell him. Important he knows."

"Captain Walters?"

"Yes. Sure to tell him. Important." Curpwell gasped, a giant gulp of air.

"Curpwell, I've got to know something. Mafia guys came after me too. Did you send them?"

"No. Don't know about it."

"Do you know who's behind the earthquakes?"

"No."

"Where did this Musso go?"

"Go? Musso? Oh." His face twisted as he remembered something important. "Think they went to see Professor Forben . . . er . . . Doctor Quake. They said. Stop them. They'll kill him." He gasped in air again, but his voice gurgled and cracked, rattling in his throat. He slumped forward.

Remo stopped massaging his chest. There was nothing more to do. He slowly placed Curpwell's head back against the seat. Then Curpwell spoke again.

"Remo. Tell me truth. You from the government?"

Remo leaned close to his ear again. "Yes," he said.

"Good," Curpwell said, trying to crack a smile past the dried blood on his face. "Must stop earthquake people. Don't let Mafia get hands on it."

"Don't worry, Les. I won't."

Curpwell died against Remo's hand, a small smile hardened on his bloody punctured face. Remo gently lay his head down on the desk.

The secretary was still on the telephone when he stepped out of the office. "You can slow down," he said. "No hurry now."

Remo had dropped the Cadillac at his house when he let Chiun off. Down in front now, he got back into his rented red hardtop, gunned the engine, and sped off toward the hills overlooking the valley, where he knew the Richter Institute was. His ears picked up the sound of sirens behind him. It would be the doctor. Maybe Wyatt.

So he had been wrong. It wasn't Curpwell. One innocent man dead, and maybe Remo—by refusing to pay the quake insurance, by accusing Curpwell of being behind it—maybe Remo had played a part in getting him killed. Now there was Doctor Quake to worry about.

Outside the town, the black roadway suddenly became bare of curbing, then the occasional gas stations and car washes vanished. The roadway was bare and heat-soaked, sending up waves that shimmered and made the road ahead always look wet.

Off to the side, Remo saw a glass encased telephone booth.

He pulled up to it, skidding dirt and rocks as he veered off onto the shoulder. He jammed on his brakes and hopped out through the passenger's door. He glanced at his watch. About noon. Smith should be there.

He dialed the direct 800 area code number that went to Smith from anywhere.

It was answered on the first ring.

"Smith."

"Remo."

"What's happened?"

"A man named Curpwell was killed. The Mafia's in on this now. They tried to get him to talk about the quakes. Another gang of Mafia goons tried to kill me and Chiun today."

"The Mafia," Smith said, as if repeating to himself the latest chess move in an opening unfamiliar to him. "The Mafia, hmmmm."

"Goddamit, Dr. Smith, stop muttering to yourself."

"Under no circumstances must the Mafia get its hands on the earthquake people before we do."

114

"I know that," Remo said heatedly. "One thing."

"What?"

"Before Curpwell died, he said I should tell a Captain Walters of the state police that the Mafia was interested in earthquakes."

Smith interrupted him. "You can forget it."

"Why?"

"Because Captain Walters is one of our men. So was Curpwell. They didn't know it, of course, but they worked for us. Walters was the next man in the chain above Curpwell. You've delivered the message, so forget Walters."

"Why the hell didn't you tell me Curpwell was one of ours?"

"I didn't want to inhibit you," Smith said.

"You've sure inhibited him. He's dead."

Smith ignored him. "Where are you going now?"

"I think those goons might be going to see Dr. Quake. I'm going there."

"Be careful."

"Right sweetheart. I'd hate for you to have to go through the trouble of requisitioning a flag for my funeral."

Remo hung up and jumped back into the car. Seconds later, it was roaring at top speed along the highway, nearing the mountains at the base of which was the Richter Institute.

So Curpwell was one of ours. And the Mafia moving its clumsy paws into the earthquake picture could end up burying an entire state by accident—a grave from Oregon to Mexico. Remo had to get to the quake makers first.

# CHAPTER SEVENTEEN

The Richter Institute was nestled back on a small shelf hollowed out of the San Bernardino mountains. It was a small, one-story red brick building nestled in under an overhang of rock and it looked like California's 1970 version of the little one-room school.

From the road that circled around below, the building was not visible, but signs brought the traveler up a grade, over a wooden bridge that Remo felt was awfully loose and up onto the shelf. Remo pulled his red hardtop to the edge of the shelf and looked down.

There, only thirty feet below him, lay the San Andreas Fault, the time bomb that ticked away under California. The earth was broken and cracked there. Remo remembered from his geology texts the aerial views that showed the fault to be an almost perfectly straight line separating the two "plates" which cut through California. There was one flaw in the straight line. The Richter Institute was built right here, right on the bend in the fault, the spot where the fault was locked and had been for fifty years, building up pressure that could blow at anytime, tearing California apart.

At that moment, Remo realized why the bridge to the shelf had been so loose. It was designed that way so that it would drift if there were an earth tremor. A solidly anchored bridge might be destroyed.

Down around the bend of the shelf, near the fault below, Remo could see a pair of pipes jutting up from the ground. Near them was a small trailer-cabin, a Volkswagen bus parked in front of it. Remo craned his neck and looked left. Far away in the distance was another pair of pipes, barely perceptible at this distance, even to his eyes.

Remo put the car in gear and burned rubber, heading up toward the institute building.

There was only one car in front, a dark blue Cadillac brougham, and Remo pulled up alongside it. He reached out to feel its hood. The car was still hot—too hot for sitting in the shade. The Mafia men had not been here long. And Remo entertained for a moment the idea that there was an easy way to get rid of the Mafia: stop making Cadillacs. He'd have to be sure to mention it to Dr. Smith.

There was only one door into the building. Remo pushed it open, then stood inside the coolness for a moment, listening. His ears picked up the sound of voices to his left. He turned that way down a long corridor that ran along the front of the building, with all the offices on its right.

One door was open and Remo walked in. He was in a laboratory, a large open room illuminated brightly by overhead lights, the lights glinting off the glass and chrome tables on which there were rows and rows of test tubes, piles of dirt and stone.

In one corner of the room, there was a computer console that covered almost half the wall. Its tapes whirred softly as they spun. Multi-colored lights flashed on and off and dials pulsated with information gathered from God knew where.

The voices came from a door alongside the computer and Remo stepped toward the door to listen in. The voices were muffled by the rhythmic thumping of some kind of machinery; Remo strained to listen.

A harsh voice said: "Forget that scientific jazz. How do you make an earthquake? That's all we want to know."

And the deepest voice Remo had ever heard answered, the words coming so slowly that it seemed to take all the speaker's energy to drop his voice into the basement of his throat, "But you can't do it without science, don't you see?"

"Well, just tell us how you do it."

"I *don't* do it. But it could be done." The voice ponderously moved on. "Now try to understand. Along the different fault systems—a fault is a break in the earth—pressure builds up along the crack. When the pressure gets too great, there is an earthquake. Now what could be done—mind you, *could* be done— would be to relieve some of this pressure before it builds so high that it must blow. It's rather like boiling water on a covered pot on the stove. If you tilt the cover up slightly, it releases the pressure and then the water doesn't boil over or the cover blow off. It's the same principle."

"All right, all right. How do you relieve the pressure?"

"No one can yet. I've been trying to develop a new kind of pump that would use water pressure to do it. That would make many small tremors to relieve pressure slowly and thus prevent a big quake. But the work is slow, particularly since the government cut off my research funds. I don't know if it will ever be done."

There was a long pause. Then the first voice said, "Dr. Quake, I don't believe you. Somebody out here is making earthquakes. You're either doing it or you know who's doing it. Now you're going to tell us about it or we'll make you wish you had."

"I don't believe that you're really from the FBI," came Dr. Quake's voice of doom.

"You're very smart, professor. Now if you're really smart, you'll tell us what we want to know."

All right. Time, Remo thought.

He stepped in through the partially opened door. "Good afternoon, professor," he said, smiling stupidly. There were only three men and it took no imagination at all to pick Dr. Quake. He was a heavy man, not really fat, but heavy, wrapped in a tweed jacket and pants that matched neither each other nor him. His face was a perfect sphere and an electric shock of graying black hair ran halfway down his forehead, where it met the upward thrust of a giant set of iron-gray eyebrows that splayed in all directions like frozen splashes of hair, shooting up to the sides and down over his metal-rimmed glasses. He was sitting on a high stool next to the laboratory table. The other two men were standing. They were young, Mafia types.

A typical Mafia pair. One looked as if he had an IQ of seven. The other looked intelligent enough, but had all the facial character of the third boy from the left in the road production of Guys and Dolls.

IQ Seven turned to Quake. "Who the hell is this creep?" he said, nodding his head in derision at Remo, who still wore the white trousers, shirt and sneakers of the morning.

"I'm Remo Blomberg, the professor's assistant," Remo said. "Professor, there's no point in trying to fool these men any longer. I think, yes, I truly think that we should give them the secret of the earthquakes."

120

The two Mafia men stared at Remo and did not notice Dr. Quake start to say "but . . .".

Remo talked to the two men directly. "It's a new machine we've invented," raising his voice to carry over the steady thumping that filled the room. "We call it the Modified Mercalli Intensity Scalerizer." So much for Smith's geology textbooks.

"Yeah?" said the smart one. "Well, how do you work it?"

"It works off Vitamin E compound. You treat the ground as if it were a yeast, you see, and you pump it full of carbon dioxide. This creates a gaseous imbalance. Then you inject large quantities of Vitamin E—not the stuff you buy in the drugstore, of course—but real, power-packed Vitamin E. And you pump it into the fissures with pneumatic ninja shots. It relieves the gaseous imbalance and you have an earthquake. It's really quite simple," he said, bending over, playing with the crease of his pants, trying not to laugh.

He looked up. "Anyone can work it. A geological belch. We've caused a few minor earthquakes with it, already. Do you want to buy one? Got a town you want destroyed?"

The two hoodlums were confused now. Their instructions obviously did not carry this far. They looked at each other, then the smarter one spoke again: "We want to see it first."

Remo addressed Dr. Quake. "Professor. There's really no use in not cooperating. I'll show them the Mercalli Scalerizer." That's two for Smith. Remo was fast becoming a convert to the cause of education.

Remo turned to go back through the door. Get them away from Quake. The one hood who had done all the talking waved at the professor. "You stay put,

Professor, and don't try anything stupid. We're not forgetting that you tried to lie to us. We'll be back."

The two men followed Remo who led them through the next laboratory and out into the hall. Remo heard one of them say: "Blomberg, eh? Trust a Jew to know when to play ball."

Remo led them down the stone hall toward the other end of the building, looking for a door that was sure to be open. To his left, he saw one slightly ajar.

"It's in here, men," he said, waving his arm to the left. He pushed open the door and walked in, the two men right at his heels.

He was in a small kitchen.

"This is a kitchen," one man said.

"That's right," Remo said. "We keep it in the refrigerator. You don't think we'd leave it laying around where prying eyes could see it, do you?"

He opened the refrigerator door and beckoned the two men closer. "There it is," he said, pointing with a royal index finger into the bowels of the refrigerator where a quarter-pound stick of margarine sat on a red saucer. The two men stepped forward. A step, two steps, then around the door and in front of the refrigerator. Remo went up in the air and came down with an elbow on the top of the skull of the one who had yet to speak a word; the skull went all soft and mushy under his elbow, then the man dropped to the floor.

Remo was behind the second man, his right hand around the back of the man's neck, his fingers like talons, biting into the clusters of the nerves. The man screamed. His arms were extended rigidly at his sides, frozen there by pain.

"All right," Remo said. "Which one of you is Musso?"

He relieved the pressure a little so the man could answer.

He gasped. "Musso ain't here. He went back. He told us to call him later and tell him what we found out."

Remo squeezed again. "Which one killed Curpwell?" then released the pressure and the man hissed, "Musso did. With an icepick. That's how he works."

"What are you guys after?" Remo asked.

The man's arms were still extended stiffly at his sides. He answered: "Somebody's making earthquakes and shaking down people. Don Fiavorante sent Musso to find out about it."

"Don Fiavorante?"

"Yeah. Pubescio. He's the head man."

"What's your name?"

"Festa. Sammy Festa," the man snivelled.

"All right, Sammy. I'm going to let you live. For awhile." He squeezed harder again. "You go back. You tell Musso and you tell Pubescio that they stay away. Tell them to forget earthquakes if they know what's good for them. Tell them to stay away from Doctor Quake. Tell them if they come back to San Aquino County, they're going out in a doggy bag. Especially Musso. You tell him that." He squeezed even harder. "You got that?"

"I got it. I got it."

Remo released his grip on the man's neck and Festa made a clumsy move for a gun under his jacket. He wheeled toward Remo. Then Remo's hand was around Festa's and around the gun.

"That Cadillac got power steering?"

"Yeah."

"Then you can drive it with one hand?"

"Yeah."

"Good," Remo said and with his right hand, frac-

123

tured Festa's forearm. The gun clattered on the floor. Festa screamed with pain, then looked down at the gun, then up at Remo.

Remo was smiling. "Remember to tell Musso what I said. My name is Remo. He may want to know that."

Festa clutched his broken arm, pain contorting his pretty-boy features. "I'm sure he's gonna want to know that."

"Be sure to tell him. Remember, my name is Remo. Now get out of here, before I change my mind."

Festa was out the front door before Remo reached the corridor. When Remo passed the front door, he saw the Cadillac swerving back out of its parking space and speeding away from the institute.

Good. That'll bring Musso back. Remo wanted him . . . for Curpwell. But his chief job was to track down the earthquake people and he couldn't spend time on side trips. But if Musso came back? Well, not even Smith could complain if Remo defended himself. After all, what else can you do against a man with an icepick?

· · ·

Doctor Quake was still seated at the high stool in his laboratory office when Remo returned.

The infernal machine in the corner was still running, filling the laboratory with thumping, and Remo said: "Can't you turn that damn thing off?"

"No," Quake said. "It's an endurance test. It's been running for three days. The goal is a whole week. You know, I don't think they were from the FBI at all."

"They weren't," Remo said. "Mafia."

"Mafia? Oh, dear. What would they want with me?" Dr. Quake's eyebrows lifted, as if with a life of

124

their own. When they lowered, they threatened to cover his entire eyeball.

"They want to know how to make earthquakes. Someone around here knows how and those two goons thought it was you."

"Two? Oh yes, two. But there were four before."

"Four? What happened to the others?"

"They went off with my girls. The laboratory assistants."

"Now where the hell did they go?," Remo asked. "The girls might be hurt." He was worried now.

Then another voice came. "We're not hurt."

Remo turned behind him, toward the door, and his eyes opened wider. Two girls stood there, perhaps in their early 20's. They wore identical clothing, white tee shirts with a clenched red fist on them and the imprint N.O.W., and blue jeans. But that wasn't what caught Remo's eye.

What caught Remo's eye was the extraordinary breasts on both of them. They were bra-less, but their breasts were firm and vibrant, and so large that they intimidated the fabric of the tee-shirts they wore. Remo thought of the two girls instantly as the eighth and ninth wonders of the world. Or considering two each, the eighth, ninth, tenth and eleventh wonders of the world.

Only as an afterthought did Remo look at their faces, alabaster white and lovely under jet-black hair—which proved that Remo had been in California too long because he regarded as an oddity any girl who wasn't blonde and tanned. He thought all this, then realized the girls were identical twins.

"Are you all right, daddy?" one of them asked, and they walked up to Doctor Quake's side, boobs a-jiggle, bubbly and bouncy under the tee shirts, butts awobble under the tight blue jeans. Reno felt a sudden lust that he told himself was sick and degenerate, then leaned back to savor.

He sat back onto a chair, crossed his legs discreetly, and if he had it in him to blush, he would have blushed.

Imagine. Two of them looking like that.

One girl put a hand on Dr. Quake's shoulder. "We were worried," she said.

"Oh, no. Nothing to worry about. This gentleman here saw to that."

Both girls now looked closely at Remo and one stepped toward his side, and stood next to his chair.

Remo said, "But we were worried about you. Those were Mafia guys, you know. What happened to the two you were with?"

The girl by Quake hesitated. Then she said, "They left."

"Without their car?"

The girl looked confused. The girl by Remo's side spoke up. "They decided to stretch their legs and walk. They said their friends would pick them up along the road." The other girl giggled. Obviously, she thought that was funny.

"Oh," Remo said.

"By the way," said the girl standing next to Dr. Quake, "who are you?"

"Name's Remo. Remo Blomberg." He tried to force his eyes to her face, tried to meet her eyes, tried desperately to look at something beside her breasts.

He was not successful. If he had been, he would have seen surprise. Instead, he saw only bosom. The girl next to Remo moved even closer to him, then put her hand on the back of his chair. She was only a bite away, throbbing and pulsating with each heart beat and breath.

"What are your names?" Remo said.

"I'm sorry," Doctor Quake said. "These are my two daughters. They assist me. This is Jacki and that's Jill."

Remo looked up at the girl next to him and caught her eyes past the edge of her bosom.

"Jacki and Jill," he said. "That's cutesy poo."

The girl leaned down close to his ear. "Would it be cutesy-poo if I grabbed you and squeezed?" she whispered.

"No," Remo said. "That would be a no-no. Or, maybe a no-no no-no," he said, recalculating his arithmetic.

"They're identical twins," Doctor Quake said, belatedly and unnecessarily.

Remo nodded, then to the girl at his side, he said softly: "You're not really identical."

"No?"

"No. I make you out to be a 42-D. I figure she's only a 41½."

"Mother always liked me best," Jill said, then added, "I didn't think you'd notice."

"Yeah. And if you put me in the Sistine Chapel, I wouldn't look at the ceiling."

"A lot of men don't. In California, anyway. You know how they are. I thought maybe you."

"Don't let the sailor suit fool you," Remo said. Then louder, "What is it you do here?"

Remo had addressed the question to Quake, but the scientist's head was turned, looking over toward the corner from which the steady thumping sound came.

Remo repeated the question, this time to the girls. "What is it you do here?"

"If you can stand up without embarrassing yourself," said 41½D at Doctor Quake's shoulder, "we'll show you."

Inhale. Heavy on the oxygen. Drain blood out of the groin. Flood the lungs, the brain. Think of fields of daises . . . daisies. It took Remo a split second and he was able to stand almost straight up.

"The power of negative thinking," he pronounced. Then Jill, standing next to him, put her hand on the small of his back.

Remo sat down again. "On second thought, why don't you tell me about it while I sit here? I'm rather comfortable."

He crossed his legs awkwardly.

"Don't be embarrassed," Jill said, whispering hotly in his ear. "We do that to people sometimes." Her hot breath didn't help. Neither did her left breast laying heavily on his shoulder.

"You're like a pornographer's daydream," Remo said. "Go ahead. I'll give you a headstart."

Jill walked away from Remo to the far corner of the room where the machine thumped away. Carefully and with great effort, Remo arose and followed her. Jacki's eyes played with Remo as he passed her, and then she followed him. Doctor Quake brought up the rear.

"This is daddy's invention. The way we're going to make the world earthquake proof," Jill said, pointing to the machine on the table. It was the size and shape of a five-gallon gas can and was painted bright blue.

"What is it?" Remo asked.

"Well, you could call it a water laser."

"A water laser?" Remo's mind shuffled through the one percent of the geology book that he still remembered.

Then, "I never heard of such a thing."

"Of course not. It's still experimental." Jacki's voice came from over Remo's shoulder.

"What does it do?"

Jill answered. "You've seen light lasers, which intensify the power of light by amplifying their waves. You know. Lasers can cut stone and metal. Even diamonds. Well, the professor has done the same thing with water. Water flows in a wave pattern, crests and troughs. Doctor Quake has smoothed out the waves, so that the force is steady—no pulsations and no vibration. This machine will be able to focus a flow of water into a stream of tremendous power."

"What has that got to do with earthquakes?" Remo asked, forgetting Jill's boobs for the moment.

Dr. Quake spoke up, in that funereal, words-of-God voice. "The San Andreas fault is six hundred miles long, Mr. Blomberg. Every mile along the fault, we have drilled and dropped shafts. These shafts are loaded with sensors—to measure heat, pressure and other things, too—and their readings are recorded back on the computer in the other room.

"With constant monitoring, we can tell when the pressure on one side of the fault is building higher than the pressure on the other side. That's the pressure that creates an earthquake as nature tries to equalize the pressure."

He stopped as if he had answered Remo's question.

"Yes," Remo said. "But what does this machine have to do with earthquakes?"

"Oh, yes. The water-laser. Well, by hooking this device up to those shafts before the pressure reaches a critical point, we could pour water pressure down into the fault. The tremendous power of the water surge will literally force the rock apart, with only a modest tremor. But it relieves the pressure instantly and can prevent a major earthquake."

"If it works," Remo said, "That's a great invention."

"Oh, it works," said Jacki, standing alongside Dr. Quake. "We know it works. But do you think we can convince your idiotic government that they should assist us with our research? No," she hissed. "They'd rather be building bombs and spending billions to mess up people's lives in Asia. And the Professor has had to struggle along without funds."

"Without funds?" Remo said. "Somebody built the building. Somebody pays your salaries."

Jill interrupted. "Friends," she said. "Donations from people and foundations that understand the importance of our work. Without them, we never would have gotten this far."

"How far?"

"Far enough to test the device," Jill said. "And it works. At least, theoretically. What we have to do now is to improve our water-laser. Its power and its endurance." She thumped her hand on the side of the blue metal pump. As she hit it, her breasts jiggled under her thin tee shirt.

She smiled at Remo. "Like a demonstration?" she said.

"Anytime," he said, and then realized she was talking of the water-laser. "Sure," he said.

From a pitcher on the table, she poured a small glass of water. "Mind you," she said. "This model's just experimental. But it shows the principle."

She turned off the motor and the laboratory rang with the sudden silence. She lifted off the top of the water-laser and poured in the glass of water. "The device uses its own internal water supply," she explained.

From the side of the water-laser, there was a nozzle similar to a spout on a gas can. She began to twist a knurled nut. "I'm narrowing the stream," she said. "It's adjustable."

She turned the laser so the spout faced Remo. From the table, she picked up a steel plate, twelve inches square, and handed it to Remo. "Hold it in front of the spout," she said. "And brace yourself."

Remo took a good grip on the steel plate and held it in front of the spout. Just one cup of water. How much force could be generated from one cup of water?

Jill tossed a switch and the pump began to groan again. Remo could hear it churning and could tell by its rising pitch that it was building up to top power. And then he was almost lifted off his feet, as a jet of water shot from the front of the water-laser, smashing against the steel plate. His arms were rigid and Remo had gripped the plate with all his strength, but the force of the water acted as a battering ram and knocked Remo five feet backwards.

Remo's arms throbbed with the pressure of the water against the plate, and then the pressure suddenly stopped as the machine stepped itself down, resuming a steady, low throb.

Jill laughed at the look on Remo's face.

"I'm impressed," Remo said.

"The secret is the lack of wave pattern in the water," Jill said. "There's no surge, just a steady force. If we focus a stream of water to a narrow extreme it can cut through metal. If we use a wide stream, it can crush. You just saw us use a cup of water. The water-laser holds five gallons when it's full."

She turned a dial and the machine slowed down even more. "We're testing it now for endurance," she said.

"And this is the only one?" Remo asked.

She paused. "Yes. The only one. Why?"

"Because I think someone may have stolen your plans. Do you know that someone is able to cause earthquakes and is trying to shake down people in this area for protection money?"

131

"Well, they couldn't do it with this machine. It's too small. Still experimental," Jill said. "And as for stealing our plans, there are no plans. We built the water-laser from scratch, improvising as we went. And who'd be crazy enough to make an earthquake?"

"Who indeed?" Jacki snorted, behind Remo.

"If enough money's involved," Remo said, "you can find somebody crazy enough to do anything. That's why your Mafia friends were here today. They're trying to move in."

"Are you a detective, Remo?" Jill asked. "You seem very concerned."

"A detective? No thanks. I'm just a store owner trying to make a living and I'm not going to be able to if I have to pay shakedown money."

Dr. Quake walked away and sat himself down behind a desk, looking through a sheaf of papers.

"Listen," Remo said softly to the girls. "I think you ought to get a guard here or something. Until this whole thing is cleared up. The Mafia might be back."

"Oh, I think that's silly," Jill said. "By the way, what happened to those two men who were here? What did you tell them? We saw them driving away in a real hurry."

"Only one drove away. The other one's dead in your kitchen."

"Dead?"

"Dead."

She started to say something, then stopped. She turned to walk away. "If you haven't any more questions, Remo, we've got work to do."

"Sure thing," Remo said. "We'll talk again. Why don't you stop sometime and have a swim in my pool?"

"Maybe we will," Jill said.

"I'm sure we will," Jacki said.

# CHAPTER EIGHTEEN

Wade Wyatt was standing alongside the road, throwing up Gertie's lunch into a ditch.

Remo saw the black and white sheriff's car on the side of the road as he drove back from the institute. Speed-trap, he thought. But as he drew abreast of the star-studded patrol car, he saw Wyatt at the side, his burly back heaving spastically as he upchucked. Next to Wyatt was a cadaverously thin man, dressed in the same tan uniform as Wyatt. The deputy, Remo remembered.

Remo pulled off onto the shoulder of the road, left the motor running, and got out. He walked back to Wyatt, who was still heaving.

"Must be something you ate, sheriff," he said pleasantly.

Wyatt turned. "Oh, it's you." He pointed down into the ditch and resumed vomiting.

Remo looked down. Two men were at the bottom of the ditch. They wore blue suits and had elaborate hair styles that would delight a hair spray manufacturer. It looked as if the two of them had choked on their intestines. Gobs of guts were stringing from their mouths as if their stomachs had been crushed and their intestines had taken the only way out, through their mouths.

"Man," Remo said, "they must eat in the same place you do."

Wyatt had his stomach under control now. His deputy said to Remo, "Don't be talking to the sheriff that way."

"I'm a taxpayer, sonny," Remo said.

"Even a taxpayer got no right to go mouthing off to Sheriff Wyatt that way."

"Sorry," Remo said. "No offense."

"All right," the deputy said. "Just so's you know."

Wyatt hitched up his pants and slid down into the ditch.

"Who are they, sheriff?" Remo asked.

"Don't know yet. Ginzos. Eye-talians," he explained. "Wouldn't surprise me none if these were the wops that killed Curpwell."

"Good thinking," said Remo who knew better. "Who found the bodies?"

Wyatt was now reaching a hand delicately into the first man's pocket, looking for a wallet.

"Phone call from a motorist," he said.

Satisfied the first man's pockets were empty, Wyatt began to look through the second man's clothes. Nothing there, either. As he stood up, Remo noticed that the men's trouser flies were open. He noticed something else too. Around their waists, their shirts and trousers were slightly discolored. As if they had been wet, and then baked dry quickly by the sun.

Wyatt clambered to the roadway again. Almost to himself, he said, "Two unidentified white males. Hit and run victims."

"Hit and run?" Remo said. "I never saw anybody hit by a car who looked like that."

"Yeah? What do you know about it? You seem to know a lot about a lot of things." Wyatt said.

"Nothing," Remo said. "Sorry to interfere."

"Yeah. You're big on interfering. First at Curpwell's office. Now here. We're going to have to talk about that," Wyatt said menacingly.

"Well, I'll get out of your way then and let you do your job," Remo said. "By the way, sheriff, one thing?"

"What's that?"

"You know anyplace in town where I can get raw oysters? You know, all slippery and slimy on the half shell?"

Wyatt spun and began upchucking again.

"Guess not," Remo said to the deputy and walked away.

"Fagola," Wyatt hissed after Remo's car departed and then heaved some more. It was not the idea of raw oysters that had made him chuck and not even the sight of the two mutilated bodies. He had seen men die like that before. Weinstein and McAndrew.

What upset Sheriff Wade Wyatt's stomach was the phone call he had received. The young female voice had told him where to find the bodies and had done something else too. She had summoned him to a meeting that night. And that could mean only trouble.

# CHAPTER NINETEN

"Remo. Remo. Remo."

Don Fiavorante Pubescio slammed the telephone receiver back onto its stand.

"Always Remo. Is my life to be destroyed by some department store owner?"

He looked down at Manny the Pick Musso, who sat sweating unhappily in a canvas sling chair next to Don Fiavorante's swimming pool.

"I am unhappy with you, Emanuel," Pubescio said. "Very unhappy."

Musso extended his hands to his sides, palms up, and shrugged. He tried a smile that was meant to be ingratiating but turned out to be sickly.

"That was Gromucci on the telephone. Gummo is dead. Albanese is dead. Palermo is dead. Killed by this Remo, whoever he is. And you!"

"I send you to find out something about earthquakes. You wind up killing a man. Then instead of doing the job right, you come back and let your men go talk to that professor. And now two of your men are missing. One of your men is dead. Another one has a broken arm. Why? Because of this Remo."

He leaned over, tall and tanned in a pale flowered bathing suit, shook a finger into Musso's sweating face.

"Do you know what is wrong, Emanuel? I will

tell you what is wrong. I like people too much. I put my trust and my faith in fools. I trust Gummo to straighten out a little labor problem at a grape farm. It is too much for him. He is dead.

"I trust you to find out a little piece of information for me. Do you do it? No. It is too much for you, so you come back here with your tail between your legs.

"Why? Because of somebody named Remo."

Pubescio turned and walked toward the edge of the pool, then turned back to speak again.

"What should I do with you, Emanuel?"

Musso opened his mouth to speak, then closed it as Pubescio went on.

"Should I do what they did in the old days, to punish failure? I would have cause. No one could point a finger at me and say there is Don Fiavorante Pubescio, who treats his men unfairly and in anger. No one could say that, should I do what I have a right to do. But, no, I am too kind. I like you too much. So I will tell you something.

"This Remo is not just a department store owner. What he is, I do not know. But what he is not, I know. And what he is not is just a shopkeeper. Somehow, he is involved with the earthquake people. He knows about it and he can tell us what we want to know.

"But will he tell us if we walk up to him and say, 'Hey, Mister Remo, tell us about the earthquake people?' No, he will not tell us that way. He will tell us if he is forced to tell us. He will tell us only to stop the pain.

"Now, do I have a man who can inflict this kind of pain? Yesterday, I would have answered: 'Yes. I have Emanuel Musso. He is just the man for the job.' But today, I am no longer sure. Perhaps Emanuel Musso has grown soft. Perhaps he has become too old for his job. Perhaps I should seek a younger, stronger man."

Musso stood up from the sling chair. "Don Fiavorante, I am not too old or too soft and so I ask a favor. Send me after this Remo. We will make him talk, my friend and I," he said, patting his jacket pocket where his icepick was jammed into a cork.

"You ask to go? You ask to go after a man who has told you never to reappear or you will be carried out feet first?"

"I ask to go."

"Perhaps you are still the Emanuel Musso of the old days. Perhaps you are ready to gamble all on your skills. Because this is a second chance and there is no third chance." He looked searchingly into Musso's eyes to make sure that Musso had understood. Succeed this time or chips out of the game.

Musso understood. "I will not fail, Don Fiavorante. I will get the information you seek. And then I will repay this Remo for his insolence to you. I will teach him a very painful and enduring lesson. After all, he is only a man, isn't he?"

Don Fiavorante Pubescio did not answer. He flexed his legs, dove into his pool and began to swim its length underwater.

# CHAPTER TWENTY

Sheriff Wade Wyatt was going to have to deliver a message to Washington. An important message.

"Shoot," he said. "I don't know nobody in Washington."

"Then ask John Wayne for an introduction, pig. We don't care how you do it."

The girl who spoke to Wyatt across the living room of the small trailer wore blue jeans that stretched taut over the muscles of her buttocks and legs as she walked. She was naked from the waist up and the nipples of her enormous breasts played peekaboo through her long, swirling black hair.

Wyatt licked his lips.

"Sheriff, I do believe you're thinking impure thoughts," she said. She stepped closer to Wyatt who sat in a straightbacked wooden chair with no cushion. It was uncomfortable on his butt and he felt like a schoolboy at a desk, being scolded by his teacher.

She stopped in front of him and flung her hair back behind her with a toss of her head. The rising mounds of her breasts stared back at Wyatt's staring eyes.

"Like them, sheriff?" she taunted. "Like them?" she demanded.

"Yes," he sputtered.

"Well, don't touch, pig. Not if you want to stay alive. You know what happens to men who touch.

Feinstein. McAndrew. The two Mafia goons. They liked them too. You want to wind up like that?"

"Nope." said Wyatt promptly and honestly.

"Okay. Then keep your fly zippered and your lip buttoned. I don't know what you're so upset about anyway. We're going to make you a rich man."

"I don't want to be a rich man. I just want to be a good sheriff."

"You were precluded from being a good sheriff the instant the sperm hit the egg. And if you worried so much about being a good sheriff, you should have thought of that before you took that girl to the motel. Before you posed for all those nice dirty pictures that we've got of you. You know, pig, you do what we want you to, just so we don't send those pictures around. We're just cutting you in on the money because we like you. We really do. You're a sweet guy. For a pig."

She turned and walked back to the sofa and lay down on it. Her giant globes flattened against her chest and she began idly to inspect her nipples as she spoke.

"First, Washington got involved by sending McAndrew. And we warned them, no more. And then they send this Remo Blomberg."

"*That fairy?* A government man?"

"Yes, with your usual perception, you would think he was a fairy, wouldn't you? Well, now you're going to get a message to Washington. You're going to tell them that because they keep sending people in here, it's going to cost them. Exactly one million dollars. Small, used bills. Not in sequence. And they're going to give the money to you. And you're going to bring it here and put it in that refrigerator.

"And this is going to be the last money delivery for you. And to celebrate we've got a big bonus for you.

You could use $25,000, couldn't you? You could buy a matched set of pearl-handled revolvers. A genuine gold statuette of the raising of the flag at Mount Suribachi. Lapel flag pins for all your friends. Season tickets for the gas chamber."

She rolled onto her side, her breasts preceding her by a split second and looked at Wyatt. "Unless you don't want that," she said. "Unless you want those nice photographs of you in the motel being sent to every home in San Aquino. You want that instead?"

Wyatt swallowed. His seat was really uncomfortable now. "No, I don't want that. You know that. But how'm I going to convince anybody in Washington to listen to me?"

"If you had even the brain that's normal for a pig, you'd figure that out. I've told you that Remo Blomberg is a government man. So call him. Tell him. He'll get the message to the government for you and he'll get the money for you. Oh, and another thing you can tell them is that we're going to give them a little taste tomorrow. An earthquake. Not a big one. Just a little number eight on the scale. But if we don't get the million, we're going to give them the works. We'll rip California right off the continent."

"Should I tell that to this Jewboy, Blomberg?"

"Yes. And make sure that's all you tell him. You mention us and you'll wind up in a ditch sucking your own guts."

"Should I kill him after I get the money?"

"That order's cancelled, pig, because frankly we don't think you're man enough to. We're going to take care of him ourselves."

"The usual way?"

"The usual way. We'll give him some pleasant memories to carry to the grave."

"The poor fagola bastard," Wyatt said, clucking.

"If you screw up, it'll happen to you. But without the pleasant memories. Now I think you better get out of here. Jacki'll be back any minute and the sight of you makes her sick. Just don't forget. We want that money here tomorrow night. The quake'll be in the afternoon. Don't stand under any bridges."

Wyatt shuffled to his feet. "All right, Jill. But I don't like it."

"And I don't like your calling me Jill, as if we were friends. To you, I'm ma'am."

"Yes, ma'am. No offense intended."

"All right, pig. Beat it."

On his way back to town, Sheriff Wade Wyatt had other thoughts on his mind. It wasn't fair for a man's life to be ruined, just because he had made one mistake. How was he to know that girl in the motel had been a pro and that he was being framed with pictures? They had given him a set of the pictures. He'd be a laughing stock if anybody ever saw them. He didn't know what had gotten into him, acting the pervert like that. All that French stuff. No wonder the Frenchies didn't amount to anything. They were all sick. Sex sick.

And he hadn't even liked it. That's what made it worse.

Now the twins had the pictures and so they had Sheriff Wade Wyatt. Imagine him, working not only against his own country, but against the sovereign state of California.

He wished he knew what to do.

But she had said this was the last one. Maybe it'd be over then.

Back at his office, Wyatt put his feet up on the desk and looked at the phone a long time, before lifting it up and getting a number from information.

He dialed and the Chink answered. When the fag

Blomberg got on, the sheriff told him he had to see him right away. "Be glad to come," the fag said. "How's your stomach feeling?" he asked before hanging up.

Wyatt thought back to the afternoon. The two men in a ditch  He reached for the wastepaper basket and heaved into it.

# CHAPTER TWENTY-ONE

On his way to Wyatt's office, Remo wondered what the sheriff wanted to talk about. Probably Curpwell's death. Well. Remo would tell him nothing about that. Musso belonged to Remo. Personally.

Of course, it might not be Curpwell. Maybe it was something important. A Red plot to fluoridate the water. Schools brainwashing children.

Maybe something about the earthquake people. Somehow Quake's machine was under all this. Remo would bet on that. He couldn't wait for the chance to try extracting some information from Jacki and Jill.

He parked the red car in front of the low two-story frame building which housed a men's shop on the first floor with Wyatt's office upstairs.

Remo took the stairs two at a time. The door was open. Remo walked in without knocking.

Wyatt was sitting at his desk. He still looked puke-white, Remo thought. Maybe he'd found out someone was poisoning his food.

"Close the door, Blomberg," Wyatt said, standing up.

Remo shoved the door shut with his foot and sat in a fabric-covered chair that Wyatt waved him to. The sheriff deposited his bulk back down in his own swivel chair.

"Well, sheriff," Remo said. "What's on your mind?"

Wyatt swallowed, getting his words accurately in his mind, then hooked his thumbs under his belt loops and leaned back.

"Blomberg," he said, finally, "I don't think you're a department store owner."

"Sure, I am," Remo said. "It's the big red building down the block. I'm having the signs changed tomorrow."

"I don't mean that," Wyatt said. "I know you own the store. What I mean is, well, I think you do other work too."

"Other work?" Remo said.

"Yeah. Like I think you work for the government." He held up a hand to silence Remo. "Now I don't expect you to tell me anything, so don't say anything. But just listen, because this is important."

"All ears, sheriff," Remo said, crossing his legs at the knee.

"I got a call tonight from the quake people. They told me on the phone there's going to be a quake tomorrow. A big one. But they want me to get a message to Washington. They want a million dollars or else they'll pull a quake that'll split California ino half."

"What are you telling me for? I don't have a million dollars," Remo said.

"Well, it's like I said. I kinda think you work for the government. Now there's no way I can get that million dollar message to Washington. They're just going to think I'm some kind of California nougat. But I thought maybe you could get the message through. These people are dangerous and they're serious. They'll rip the whole state apart. Blomberg. Damn it, what I'm telling you is I need your help."

"Well, sheriff, you're wrong. I don't work for the

government. But I do have some contacts there. Some pretty important people. If you want, I could transmit the message for you."

"Well, that's something," Wyatt said. He smiled. "Maybe that'll do it."

Remo stood up. "Are you going to be here a while?" he asked.

Wyatt nodded.

Remo said, "All right, then. I'm going back to my house to make some calls. I'll call you here and let you know how I make out. By the way, who called you?"

"Called me?"

"About the quake? And the million dollars?"

"Oh, yeah. A man. Never heard his voice before," Wyatt said.

"Another by-the-way, sheriff. Any leads on who killed Curpwell?"

"From the description his secretary gave me, I think those guineas we found in the ditch mighta had something to do with it. Anyway, I'm listing it as a heart attack. Don't want to shake up the town."

"Been a busy day, sheriff. A heart attack; two hit-and-run victims; now this million dollars."

"That's not all, either," Wyatt said. "I got word today about some kind of a killing today out at the Gromucci farm. Three men, supposed to be killed by two men. One an old Chink. But I called Gromucci and he told me there wasn't nothing to it. Just a fairy tale." He looked at Remo suspiciously.

"Can't believe in fairy tales," Remo said pleasantly. "I'll call you back, sheriff."

"All right, Blomberg," Wyatt said. "And thanks. I appreciate it. You know, you're not such a bad guy after all."

When Remo left, Wyatt stared at the office door. Blomberg wasn't such a bad guy, particularly for a fairy. It was a shame what he was going to look like when the two girls were done with him.

# CHAPTER TWENTY-TWO

Dr. Harold W. Smith toyed with the 39¢ red plastic letter opener with a magnifying glass on one end as he listened to Remo on the telephone.

"All right," he said, "I understand. Do you have any leads? Anything at all?"

"Nothing. I think Quake's machine is involved. Maybe it's him. But he's kind of loose."

"If that's what you think, work on it."

"All right, I will. But what about the million?"

"Stay where you are," Smith said. "I'll call you back."

Smith hung up the phone, turned in his chair and stared out at the waters of Long Island Sound. Blackmailing the government. It was unthinkable. But duty required that he report the message to the President. It was a decision for him to make.

He turned back to the desk, opened a drawer and removed a telephone with a red dot in the handle. He picked up the phone.

In Washington, the President chased his wife from the bedroom and picked up the telephone which was kept in a dresser drawer.

He listened as Smith explained the circumstances. His reaction was immediate.

"Pay it," he told Smith.

"May I advise you, sir, that once started, blackmail

is difficult to stop? And this is nothing but blackmail."

"Doctor Smith, this is also California we're talking about. Not Texas."

"The decision is yours, of course," Smith said.

"And my decision is this. We will pay them the million dollars. And if they cancel the earthquake they have scheduled for tomorrow afternoon, we will up the ante to $1.5 million. Do you have that kind of money available?"

"Yes sir."

"All right. Then pay it."

"As you wish," Smith said. He hung up the telephone and dialed Remo's number. The President was wrong. He should not pay.

Remo picked up the phone on the first ring.

"Yes?"

"The President says we'll pay."

"That must send you up the wall," Remo said. "Is it coming out of your budget?"

"Not only out of my budget, but out of your expenses. You'll have to wear a pair of shoes more than a week now."

"Poor Chiun," Remo said. "He's going to have to go on short rations."

"Another thing," Smith said. "The President says we'll pay more if tomorrow's earthquake is cancelled."

"How much more?"

Smith could not bring himself to say it. He hesitated then said, "$1.2 million total."

"I don't know," Remo said. "I don't know if I can bring it home for a penny less than $1.5 million."

"Do whatever you have to do," Smith groused. "There'll be a bank draft of $1.5 million to your account in the San Aquino Bank tomorrow morning. Who's going to deliver the money?"

"The sheriff here. A big blowhard named Wyatt."

"It might be interesting to find out who he gives the money to," Smith said.

"Don't worry. I plan to."

"And Remo," Smith said. "Please try to get the money back."

"You're some piece of work," Remo said, as he hung up.

He looked up Wyatt's telephone number in the phone book and dialed.

Wyatt sounded like a recording. "This is the San Aquino County sheriff's office. This is Sheriff Wade Wyatt speaking."

"Remo Blomberg, sheriff. When do you expect those people to contact you again?"

"Probably in the morning."

"All right. I've heard from some people in Washington. They'll pay. And they'll pay an extra $500,000 if tomorrow's earthquake is cancelled. Do you think they'll stop it?"

"I don't know," Wyatt said. "I'll ask. How will I get the money?"

"I'll have it tomorrow," Remo said. "You can get it from me."

"Okay," Wyatt said. "They told me small, used bills, not in series."

"Right," Remo said. "I'll take care of it. And you let me know how much tomorrow."

"I'll call you as soon as I hear from them," Wyatt said.

"Okay, sheriff. Good night."

Remo hung up, glanced at his watch, and practiced his timing. When he felt a minute had passed, he looked at his watch again. Fifty-nine seconds. Not bad. He picked up the phone, dialed Wyatt's number again. The line was busy. So Wyatt was contacting them. He was probably part of it.

Well, then, tomorrow, Sheriff Wade Wyatt would get it too. Remo could not take a chance of killing him now. Not until he had the whole gang together along with whatever equipment they had. He could take no chances with a pre-set timing device that might touch off a quake.

Wyatt drummed his fingers on his desk. The phone rang eleven times before it was answered.

"This is Wyatt."

"This is Jacki. What are you calling for, pig? I told you never to call."

"It's important. Tell your sister she was right. Blomberg does work for the government. And they'll pay one and a half million if you call off tomorrow's quake."

Jacki paused for a moment, then said, "Okay, we'll do it. When are you going to get the money?"

"From Blomberg. Tomorrow afternoon."

"All right, pig. Bring it here after dark. And make sure you're not followed."

"That Blomberg tries to follow me, I'll blow him apart."

"Don't worry about him. If anybody follows you tomorrow night, it won't be Blomberg. Our friend Remo's going to be dead."

At that same moment, that very thought was in the mind of a man checking into the Cowboy Motel. His name was Musso.

# CHAPTER TWENTY-THREE

"It's all there, sheriff. A million and a half."

Wade Wyatt stood in Remo's living room, his beady little eyes peering out from under his Stetson, looking down into a brown leather valise, filled with bills.

"Small bills, old, not in series," Remo said. "Where are you going to deliver it?"

"I got to leave it tonight out on Route 17 at a special spot," Wyatt said.

"What spot?"

"Sorry, Blomberg. I can't tell you that. If I was to be followed, the whole deal'd be off. And you know what that would mean."

"Yeah, I guess so," Remo said. He was wearing a white bathing suit, having just come in from the pool to meet Wyatt. "Well, good luck," he said. "And listen. If you could get some idea of who those people are, I know folks in Washington who'd like to know."

"I'll try. You can count on that," Wyatt said, wrinkling his chin in a grimace of determination. He picked up the suitcase and left. Remo watched him walk toward his patrol car.

So much for Wyatt until nightfall. When Remo had spoken to him in the morning on the telephone, Wyatt hadn't been at all worried when Remo lied that he might not have the money until dinner-time.

So his delivery wasn't until dinner-time, at least. Reno would pick him up before that.

Remo went back through the dining room's sliding glass doors to the pool area. As he passed through the dining area, he heard the television in Chiun's bedroom blasting forth the continuing saga of Dr. Lawrence Walters, psychiatrist at large. Chiun's vice: hopeless addiction to TV soap operas.

What was it the man said about California? Remo wondered, as he lay himself down on the slate deck around the pool? The place where all the misfits of the world congregate, under the assumption that since they were going to be miserable anyway, they might as well be warm.

He'd buy that, he thought, as he felt the California sun toasting his bones. Wade Wyatt, Doctor Quake, the twins, Curpwell, the Mafia. He should write a book. About the interesting people he'd met. And the interesting people he'd killed. How many now was it? He had stopped counting. In the hundreds anyway. Just one at a time. Even the slaughter of a thousand persons begins with but a single death. Yep, he should write a book. Smith'd like that. Cut him in for part of the royalties. He'd like that better.

Remo felt himself fading away into a nap. And then he realized he was not alone.

He rolled to his side and in one motion was on his feet, his hands curled at his sides, poised on his toes.

Jacki and Jill stood there. They wore thin yellow dresses that barely reached the tops of their thighs and that hid none of their curves. They ran their eyes openly and hungrily along Remo's body; suddenly he felt naked.

"My, my, the nervous type," the one on the left commented. Remo compared her bustline carefully with her sister's. The one who spoke was Jill. She was bigger.

"And what balance," added Jacki. Remo felt foolish poised on his toes that way, in fighting position. He let himself softly down onto his feet.

"Speaking of balance," he said, "how do you two manage to stand up? It seems a violation of a natural law."

"We encourage violation," Jill answered.

"Moving violation, I hope?" Remo asked.

"There's no other kind," Jill returned. "Tell me, is this all you do? Lie around the side of the pool? Don't you swim?"

"Sometimes."

"We came to thank you . . . really thank you, for helping the professor yesterday."

"Glad to help." He fought to keep his eyes on the girls' faces. Once a tit man, always a tit man.

"Now that we're here, aren't you going to invite us in the pool?"

The girls were having that effect on him again, so Remo sat down on the edge of the low diving board.

"Sure. Help yourself."

They giggled at his discomfiture. Then, in that way known only to women and chimpanzees, they reached their arms up behind their backs and unzipped their dresses.

Slowly, they wriggled their arms from the short sleeves. The dresses fell softly on the sun-yellowed slate. They kicked off their sandals, stood there before Remo, naked, the sun glinting blue off their ebony hair, their skin creamy white as if it had never known sun. Their hips were lush, their legs long and full. Their waists were small and rising above them were the magnificent breasts, erect and full. Remo felt like

157

jumping to his feet and shouting. Except that he couldn't stand up.

These were the kind of girls, Remo thought, that men rarely dreamed about. In their dreams, men wanted beautiful women—but women who were human, who could be taken, violated, and overpowered by a man's lust. The twins in front of him now were too much for that. So ripe, rich and sensual that *they* were overpowering, a normal man would shrink from them because he would know that his lust could never conquer them. No matter how strong it was, his lust would be burned up by their sexual heat and proved inadequate.

That's how a normal man would feel. Remo was no normal man and he felt rising in him a lust beyond lust.

"Do we embarrass you?" Jill said.

"No, I like liberated women."

Jill cupped her own breasts. "Good. We like being liberated."

They approached Remo and sat down, one on each side of him on the diving board. Their hands were on his thighs, then Jacki put an arm behind his head and planted a kiss on his mouth, a long-lingering kiss in which her tongue darted into and probed his mouth.

He felt hands pulling off his bathing trunks and then his swimsuit was down around his ankles and his feet were being pulled from it. Jacki's mouth was still over Remo's and it felt as if his lungs were being sucked from him. Then he was pulled to his feet and hands were all over his body, pulling at him, feeling, stroking, rubbing. Every time he moved, he felt breasts rubbing against him, soft breasts that shuddered when his skin touched them.

Then there was no more deck and the three of them, intertwined, fell into the water. Remo felt himself being manipulated and he and Jacki were joined under the water. They broke the surface for air, then Jill plunged down and then was at Remo with her face, her tongue and lips moving. Remo planted a hand and began stroking rhythmically in the rolling waters of the pool that now slapped against the tile sides.

He felt Jill shudder spasmodically, her body releasing tension, and then Jacki pulled her mouth away from his and arched her body, crying out, "Don't stop. Don't stop."

Remo was angling them toward the pool ladder, pronging one along, pulling the other along with a fingertip, and he steered them up the ladder and followed them up, still conscious of his manhood.

"Inside," he said hoarsely.

"We're going to do you now, Remo. And do you. And do you," Jill said.

They walked toward the glass doors that opened into Remo's bedroom. Then Chiun stepped out into the poolside area. Remo felt suddenly embarrassed and stepped behind Jill before turning.

Chiun looked at the girls with distaste and at Remo with loathing.

"Oh, you're cute," Jacki said. She stepped toward Chiun. "Let's," she suggested.

He just stared at her. "Let's make it a foursome," she said.

Remo turned and went inside with Jill.

Chiun looked at Jacki coldly. "I do not perform in public," he spoke firmly.

"Shy?"

"No. I am civilized. Only cattle and beasts of the field copulate in the open."

"And liberated women," she said, sinking to her

knees in front of him, offering him her breasts. "Come on," she said. "Please. You'll never forget it."

"The last woman I had I was twelve years getting rid of," Chiun said. "I need no more slaves. Go with him. You will find him adequate in every respect. He is your type exactly."

Chiun turned and walked back into the house, heaving his shoulders in a sigh. Poor Remo. He would always be an American. Always a fancier of cows. He should have been a dairy farmer.

Jacki stood up, followed Jill and Remo into the bedroom They were already tangled together on the bed and she stood alongside them, trailing fingertips along their bodies, then she moved to join them. Jill was throbbing again and Remo felt himself being rolled off her by Jacki.

They were insatiable. It was like making love to an octopus which had come to drain his vitals, to dry him up, to turn him into an aged man in one lasting moment of lust.

Out in the living room, Chiun watched his TV tape of *As the Planet Revolves.* He watched his tape of *Edge of Dawn.* Then he stood up and turned off the television.

He heard steps behind him.

He turned.

Remo was there, buttoning a black, short-sleeved shirt. He wore black slacks and black sneakers.

"Well, little father, are you ready?" he said.

"I am always ready. And the forward ones?"

"They'll rest now," Remo said.

As they left the house, Remo saw the twins' Volkswagen bus parked at the door, behind his rented red hardtop. In the back seat of the camper was the bright blue water-laser. Stupid broads. This was probably how they were keeping it safe. By carrying it around with them.

Sure enough, the doors were unlocked. Remo saw the keys in the ignition, and pulled out the key ring, reached in and locked the doors.

"Be just a minute, Chiun," he said and walked back into the house.

He opened his bedroom door. Jacki and Jill were on the bed, unconscious, drained, exhausted, their faces wearing ecstatic smiles.

He tossed the keys toward the bed. They landed between Jill's breasts, which received them with a quiver. She smiled in her sleep at the sensation.

Remo softly closed the door and walked out. Let them sleep. They had earned it.

He whistled softly as he hurried out the front door and got into the car, where Chiun waited in the front seat. Remo moved quickly now, so quickly that he did not notice the man watching him from the front seat of a black Cadillac across the seat, cleaning his fingernails with an icepick.

# CHAPTER TWENTY-FOUR

"Chiun? How do you battle a force without vibrations?" Remo asked as they drove to town.

"There is no force without vibrations," Chiun said.

"I've seen one," Remo said. "A water-laser. It generates tremendous power, and no vibrations."

"There are always vibrations," Chiun said, "no matter how small. You must feel those vibrations, then harness them to your own until you are the master of the relationship." He folded his arms.

After a few blocks, Remo said again: "It had no vibrations."

After another block, Chiun said: "There are always vibrations. Like those you feel now. Do you feel them?"

Remo opened his senses for a moment. "Concentration?" he said.

"Yes," Chiun said. "We're being followed."

Remo looked up into the rearview mirror. The road behind them was empty. He glanced toward Chiun.

"Ahead of us now," Chiun said. "The big, black monstrosity. He just passed us and then pulled to the curb."

Remo slowed down slightly without hitting the brake, glancing at the black Cadillac in which a man sat trying to act nonchalant. Remo looked at his head, the back of his thick neck, as he drove by. Musso, he told himself.

Remo glanced at his watch. Almost six o'clock. Plenty of time before Wyatt would make his delivery. Remo hung a right on the next corner and stepped on the gas. In the mirror, he saw the black Cadillac turn the corner and follow him.

The street was thinned of people now and Remo picked up his speed, barrelling through the town, then out into the flat countryside of truck stops and gas stations. He had seen the place he was looking for the first day he'd come into town with Smith.

The Cadillac was laying back now, a car between it and Remo, and he slowed to get rid of the blocker. The station wagon behind Remo finally pulled out and passed, but the Cadillac stayed nearby, in sight. Then Remo saw the bulb-embroidered sign up ahead: "U-Du-It Car Wash."

It was a one-story cinder block building, really a tunnel open at both ends.

The road was clear both ways. Remo began to sway out into the left lane, cutting his speed and the Cadillac closed the distance between them. Remo kept slowing, watching the approaching Cadillac in the rearview mirror.

Then, just as they drew almost abreast of the car wash, Remo spun his wheel to the right. His car skidded. The Cadillac driver swerved to avoid hitting Remo and went bouncing off the roadway, turning into the gravel driveway that led to the carwash. Remo gassed his car and pulled up alongside, but slightly behind the Cadillac which was now angled in against the empty car-wash building.

"A regular Mario Andretti," Chiun said. "You must be very pleased with yourself."

Remo could tell Chiun was pleased.

"Yes, little father," he said as he opened the door and jumped out.

The driver of the Cadillac was rolling down his electric window—now he hollered out at Remo: "Hey, stupid! What's the matter? You nuts or something?"

He was a big man. Big and thick in the neck; the arm that rested on top of the door showed a heavy wrist and forearm under the sleeve of the pearl-gray suit. His face was lined and hard; his nose a slice of obsidian in his hatchet face; the kind of man, Remo thought who would kill with an icepick.

"Whyn't you watch where you're going?" Remo called coming around the front of his car. "You guys in Cadillacs think you own the road."

"Well, what'd you cut me off for?" the other driver shouted.

"Cut you off? Why, you punk," Remo shouted. "If you weren't tailgating . . . get out of that car and I'll put you on your ass!"

The door opened and Musso stepped out. "Mister," he said, "You're asking for trouble." He was big and towered over Remo.

He began to walk toward Remo, slowly, surely, and Remo began to back off. He put his hands in front of him, palms forward. "Now, just a minute, Mister. I didn't mean anything. . . ."

"Then you should learn to keep your big mouth shut," Musso said.

He kept coming. Remo was inside the opening to the car wash now, still backing up.

Musso came closer, his eyes glistening with anticipation at the fright and confusion he saw on Remo's face.

Now they were both inside the car wash; it was cool and curiously quiet. Musso reached a hand into his inside coat pocket and slowly pulled out an ice. pick whose point was jammed into a bottle cork.

He pulled the cork off, then stuck it in his side pocket. The point of the pick glistened bright and silvery in the stray glints of the late afternoon sun that angled in the front entrance of the car wash.

"Now, wait a minute, mister," Remo said. "An argument's one thing, but you've got no call to. . . ."

"Remo Blomberg," Musso said. "I have a call. I've got all the call I need. Didn't you tell one of my men that if I came back I'd go out in a doggy bag?"

He held the icepick in front of him like a street fighter's switchblade, coming on slowly now, his bulk trapping Remo and preventing escape. Remo backed up until he could see from the corners of his eyes that he was standing between the twin chains of the conveyor belt which pulled cars through the car wash.

"You're Musso?" Remo asked.

"I'm Musso."

"I've been waiting for you."

"Good," Musso said, with a smile. "Before I punch you like a railroad ticket, who's behind the earthquakes?"

"I am," Remo said. "It's my own little shakedown racket. You think I'm going to turn it over to a gang of organ-grinders?"

"That's what I thought," Musso said. Both men were still, now. Remo backed up against the damp strips of cloth hanging from the top of the car wash, marking its entrance, Musso only five feet away from him, the shiny icepick weaving back and forth. Over Musso's shoulder, Remo saw Chiun in the front seat of the car, reading a road map.

"How do you do it?" Musso said.

"I tried to tell one of your men. We do it with Vitamin E and carbon dioxide."

166

"Don't give me no smart-ass talk, Blomberg," Musso said.

"It's the truth. Ask anyone. Ask the governor. He's my partner. I took him on as second choice. I tried to interest the Mafia in it first, but they were too busy eating peppers and beating up candy store owners to give a damn. What about you, Musso? You interested? I'll cut you in for one-half of one percent. That ought to give you a fast $137 a year. It'll keep you in icepicks."

"Keep talking, Blomberg. You're digging your own grave."

Remo glanced at his watch. Time to go.

"Musso," he said. "I don't have any more time to play. The game's over."

He took a step forward toward Musso and Musso lunged with the pick. He jabbed only air, and then he saw Blomberg's hand close around the blade of the pick and it was pulled out from Musso's hand.

Then Blomberg was behind him, between Musso and his car, and he was waving the pick at Musso, who started to back off. He took one step back and then dove forward at Remo. He saw lights. Then just darkness.

Musso awakened moments later. He was sore and his back was wet. It was dark where he was and he shook his head, trying to clear his vision. He was looking up at the ceiling, lying on his back on the hood of his Cadillac.

He started to rise to a sitting position but then a hand slapped at his throat and he was knocked backward. He turned his head. There was this Remo Blomberg, still holding the pick blade, smiling at him.

"Tell me, something, Musso, did you like your work?"

"Yeah, punk."

"And how about Curpwell? You enjoy killing him?"

"Yeah. As much as anyone."

"Good. This is one for him." And then the icepick flashed up into the air and Musso closed his eyes so he wouldn't see it kill him, but it missed all his vital organs. It came down instead through his wrist, and under his wrist it punctured the steel hood of the car. Remo twisted the pick and bent it so Musso couldn't pull it out, and he was nailed there to the hood of his car like a deer in hunting season.

"Think of me in that great car wash up yonder," Remo said.

He walked away. The shock and pain from his wrist paralyzed Musso, but he turned his head and through the windshield of the Cadillac he could see Remo digging into his pocket out at the entrance to the car wash. He brought something out of his pocket—coins—and then he dropped them into a chute.

Suddenly, Musso was enveloped by a whir and then a roar. Hot water poured into his face. Soap jets shot at him, filling his nose and mouth as he tried to scream from the scalding, and he could feel bubbles forming inside his head. He wrenched and yanked, trying to pull himself free, but he could not.

He fell back and looked up. The whirring came from the overhead brushes, giant brushes, two feet in diameter; they were lowering now, coming down, only inches away, then touching Musso's face. They began to spin. He felt the first bristle flick away a gouge of skin from his face. The bristles kept turning, brushing his face, it felt like nothing more than an uncomfortable sunburn, but then the pressure came down harder and harder on him, and there was no skin left to burn, so he could feel the raw flesh stinging where the soap was jetted into it. Now he could hear his clothes ripping under the pressure of the brushes. There was more steaming hot water. Then Musso remembered nothing.

Remo waited a full ten minutes at the control panel of the car wash. Then he flipped the lever that activated the conveyor chains and the Cadillac began to lurch forward. Remo fished again into his pocket.

When his body was found the next morning, Musso would be dry and sparkling. Remo had thrown in an extra quarter to give him the special diamond-hard wax finish.

* * *

Back in the car, Chiun was still looking at the map. "Korea is not on this map," he said as Remo got behind the wheel.

"No. It's a map of California," Remo said.

"A map without Korea is no map at all," Chiun said, rolled down his window and tossed the map out onto the crushed rock driveway.

"Tell me," he added, "are you always so melodramatic?"

"Only when I know you're watching, little father," Remo said, driving away.

"Watching? Who would watch such a display?"

# CHAPTER TWENTY-FIVE

It was growing dark when they got back to town but Wyatt's black-and-white squad car was still parked in front of his office. Remo and Chiun parked across the street in a supermarket parking lot and waited.

It was almost an hour before Wyatt stepped from his front door. Remo spotted his Stetson rolling from side to side on his head as he walked around to get into his car. He still carried the brown leather valise.

Wyatt paused at his door a moment, then looked both ways before sliding in behind the wheel.

He pulled from the parking spot, drove to the end of the block and turned left, heading out of town. Remo eased out of his parking spot and fell in line, a car behind Wyatt, keeping his eyes trained on the oval stoplights on the back of the sheriff's car.

Then Wyatt turned again and he was moving out, faster now, out onto the highway leading up into the San Bernardino Mountains. It was dark now. Remo turned off his lights and drove in darkness, two hundred and fifty yards behind Wyatt.

Remo recognized the road. It was the way to the Richter Institute. So it was Dr. Quake.

Now there could be no mistake about their destination, as Wyatt turned off the main highway onto the narrow branch that led only to the shelf of mountain on which the institute was located.

Remo kept his two hundred and fifty yards distance. Then up ahead, he saw the stop-lights on Wyatt's car flash on and off as he tapped the brake, then come on to stay as he rolled to a stop. Remo quickly shifted into low, to brake the car, then into neutral and turned off the key so Wyatt could not hear the motor. He let the car roll forward, slowing it with his parking brake, finally rolling it to a stop in the darkness one hundred yards behind Wyatt.

That was odd, he thought. Wyatt had stopped short of the bridge that led up into the institute's parking area. Then Wyatt was out of the car. Instead of heading up toward the institute, he began walking along the base of the cliff. Remo remembered the trailer there. He had seen the Volkswagen bus parked in front of it the first day. It was the girls' trailer. The twins. Jacki and Jill. They were behind the quakes.

He had been a damn fool not to realize it before. Of course. They had the device. Probably had made more than one of them. Poor dumb Dr. Quake knew nothing about it. The women's libbers, they were doing it. Probably just for the dough.

He tapped Chiun on the shoulder. "Follow him," he said softly. "See what he does and where he goes. I'll meet you up there in the parking lot."

Chiun stepped away from the car, a tiny little man in a black robe. He took two steps away from the car, then vanished in the blackness of the night.

Chiun was Ninja, of the Oriental magical men who could follow a bird in flight, who could appear and disappear at will; the invisible men of the Orient. Remo knew, intellectually, that there was no magic; that it was all tricks and training. But beyond intellect, he knew too that with Chiun it was more than tricks and training. It had started that way. But it had become a magic of its own.

Wyatt whistled tunelessly to himself as he stepped heavily along the broken earth that marked the location of the San Andreas fault. Do no good to fall in, he told himself. No good at all.

And only three feet from him, but unseen, unheard, undreamed of, followed Chiun, his steps timed with Wyatt's, moving softly, sideways, not even breathing. He could have followed at a distance. A matador could have worked three feet from the bull's horns. But if he was a good one, he didn't have to. Chiun was a good one.

Remo waited and then started the motor again. As quietly as he could, he drove ahead, past Wyatt's parked car, across the wooden bridge and up into the institute's empty parking lot where he backed the car into a corner, out of sight of the roadway.

It had been the girls. And the dead men? The water-laser had been used to crush them. That was why their bodies were wet around the waist: the force of water had been used to drive their intestines from their bodies. Probably after sex, when they were too weak to resist strongly, he thought, remembering the open flies on the trousers of the men in the ditch.

Remo sat in the car, silent now, and remembered a lot of things, things he should have noticed at the start if he had been any kind of detective at all. How the girls dodged questions yesterday about the two Mafia men they had gone off with. The giggle when one said something about picking the men up "along the road."

He remembered something else too. Leaving his own house this afternoon and seeing the bright blue water-laser in the back of the girls' Volkswagen. They had come to use it on him. After they had drained and exhausted him.

He smiled to himself. Score one for Remo. As a matter of fact, score two.

He did not hear the car door open. He knew Chiun was there only when he felt the pressure of someone sitting next to him on the seat.

"Where did he go?" Remo asked.

"There is a trailer there. He carried the suitcase in and put it in the refrigerator. I took it out. Here it is."

Down below, Remo heard Wyatt's car start up and a moment later, he saw the oval tail-lights speeding down the road.

Chiun had the money on his lap. What would happen if they didn't put it back in the girls' trailer?

Let's just see, Remo said to himself.

He started the motor and drove out of the parking lot. Smith'd be happy to get his money back. And Remo would be happy to get the girls.

But when he got back to his house, the girls had gone.

# CHAPTER TWENTY-SIX

"He was the bravest man I ever met.

"He was the smartest, finest, one hundred percent American I ever met.

"He was the nemesis of all law-breakers, no matter how big or powerful they might be."

"He" was Sheriff Wade Wyatt and he was dead. He lay naked in the master bedroom of his ranch-style house, under the seven-foot square blow-up of the raising of the flag at Mount Suribachi with the photographer's name blacked out in the corner.

The bed around his midsection was soaked with water, and his entrails fought their way out of his mouth. His eyes were opened wide in deadly horror.

Looking down on the sheriff's body, working out the phrases of his eulogy, sucking on a Mary Jane, was his deputy, Brace Cole. It had not occurred to him yet that the sheriff had met a terrible death.

Cole was ready now, in case he should be asked for a statement by anyone.

So he looked around the room. He saw no clues. He looked at Sheriff Wade Wyatt's body. Just like the two guineas that they found dead in the ditch. Just like Feinstein and that geology fellow from Washington.

The men in the ditch. What was it Wyatt had said? "I wouldn't be surprised if he had something to do with this." That's what Wyatt had said and he meant that Remo Blomberg that wise-ass running that store.

Well, Sheriff Wade Wyatt befitting his grandeur as a human being had been the kind of man who would tolerate a great deal before cracking down. But not Brace Cole who was now the acting sheriff of San Aquino County, pending an election within sixty days for Wade Wyatt's unexpired term. Brace Cole was not about to let that Blomberg get away with it.

Wade Wyatt's holster hung from the bedpost and Brace Cole went over to it, then removed the .44 caliber revolver. He spun the cylinder to make sure the gun was loaded, then fingered the notches on the gun butt.

"Sheriff" he said to Wyatt's intestine-packed face, "We're going to put another notch on your gun."

Then he went out into the midnight of San Aquino County. He had not noticed the printed note on the floor near the bed, which read: "Doublecrossing American pigs. Now you pay."

Across the town, Remo sat on the blue suede sofa in his living room, talking to Smith. Chiun still wearing his black robe, sat on the dining room floor, staring through the glass windows toward the dimly-lit pool area.

"The Mafia's out of the game," Remo said. "I don't think they'll be back. But now I've got to get the girls. Quake's assistants."

"Why did they do it, do you think?"

"Who knows? They talk like radicals. More country-haters? Or maybe they just like money. Oh, speaking of money. We got yours back."

"Thank God for small favors," Smith said. "You had better get the girls before they do something dangerous."

"I will," Remo said. "We're going now."

He hung up and said, "C'mon, Chiun, let's go."

The old man rose to his feet and followed Remo out the front door. They drove from their circular driveway only four minutes before acting Sheriff Brace Cole arrived.

When he saw his prey had vanished, he broadcast a bulletin over his police radio:

"Notice to all departments in the San Aquino area. Watch for a red hardtop, rental plates being driven by one Remo Blomberg. He may be accompanied by a little Chink. Both are wanted for suspicion of murder. They are dangerous, should be considered armed and approached with caution."

Remo parked his car up in the parking area of the Richter Institute, in a corner away from casual sight. It had been a quick trip. He had been racing at full speed when a state squad car got behind him and gave him the siren but Remo lost the trooper by dousing his lights and skidding into the turnoff to the institute. He glanced back down toward the road. There was no one following him.

He and Chiun walked down a rickety flight of wooden stairs that led to the twins' trailer. The Volkswagen bus was not there. Remo and Chiun went into the trailer, to wait in the dark for the girls.

If they were going to make a quake, a big one, they'd make it someplace near here, he told himself, hoping he was right, hoping they had not just fled. This was the spot where the fault was locked, where the greatest pressure was and where their water-laser would have to be set to rip off California.

Rip off California? How many? Thirteen million people? And how many would die? A million? Two million? How many would lose their homes and their roots? Their businesses?

A million corpses. Lay them out and they'd reach halfway across the country.

Remo heard a motor, the tinny sound of a four-cylinder engine, then doors closing, then voices. He slumped down in his chair.

"The lying, thieving government. They must have had somebody follow Wyatt and steal the money." That would be Jill. "Well, now they'll pay for it."

"I don't think so." That was Jacki. "I think the big pig tried to keep the money for himself."

There was a giggle, then Jacki said, "Did you see the look on his face when we let him have the water-laser? Poor bastard. He didn't even get a chance to dip his wick." She giggled again.

They were standing now outside the trailer. "But I'd feel better if we had gotten a chance to use it on Remo. What did he do to us anyway?" Jill asked.

"I don't know," Jacki answered. "That never happened before. But I think that stupid deputy will take care of Remo. Particularly since we called him and told him that we saw Blomberg leaving Wyatt's house. When he finds Wyatt dead, he'll take care of Remo."

"Maybe," Jill said. "C'mon. We're going to set this equipment and then get out of here before the state blows. Pig government."

Remo heard footsteps walking away from the trailer, crunching twigs and leaves underfoot. He rose and peered through a window. Under the bright light of the California moon, he saw the two girls, each carrying a water-laser, walking away from the trailer, up along the edge of the fault, toward the spot where Remo knew the two drill shafts stuck up from the ground.

"Let's go, Chiun," he whispered.

"I will wait," Chiun said.

"Why?"

"Because I think it will be beneficial to wait. You go."

Remo shrugged and stepped lightly down from the trailer. What was on Chiun's inscrutable mind now? There was something.

Then Remo still clad in black, slid silently through the night following the twins.

They were twenty feet ahead of him. When they came to a large clearing they stopped. They got to work immediately beginning to hook the water-lasers together, to double their power. Then they lugged them over to the shaft that jutted up from the ground and began to fasten the coupling to the shaft.

Remo stepped out into the clearing.

"Hi, girls" he said cheerily.

They froze in position, squatting over the equipment.

"Remo," they hissed in unison.

"Yup. It was so good today, I thought I'd come back for more."

One of the girls stood up. In profile, he could tell it was Jill.

She walked slowly toward Remo, her arms extended as if in greeting. "We've thought of nothing else," she said. She licked her lips and in the moonlight they glistened black and white. Now she was at Remo; she wrapped her arms around him and pressed her breasts up close into him.

"You know what I think?" Remo said softly.

"What?" her tongue asked his ear.

"You would have made a great bull dyke."

He pushed her back and she fell to the ground. Jacki was still bent over the water-lasers and Remo headed for her. Then the ground shuddered and an explosion ripped the air. Remo was knocked off his feet. He felt a searing pain burn into his shoulder.

A voice roared over a portable bullhorn.

"Remo Blomberg! I know you're down there. This is acting Sheriff Brace Cole. You're under arrest for the murder of Sheriff Wade Wyatt. Now come on up from there or the next grenade'll land right in your lap."

Remo was stunned. The grenade had barely missed him, and he could feel a trickle of blood running down his left arm from a fragment in his shoulder.

He shook his head to clear it, then saw Jacki stand up and away from the water-lasers. The familiar thumping had started.

"Too late, pig," she said. "This whole state is going."

The water-lasers were thumping now, churning. Remo could almost feel the energy building up inside them.

"Come on, Jacki," Jill said from behind Remo. "Let's get out of here."

"Sheriff," she called. "We're coming out. Don't shoot. He's been holding us prisoner. Don't shoot."

"Come ahead," boomed the voice of Brace Cole. "I'll cover. . . ." And then his voice stopped, in mid-sentence.

Remo got to his feet. Another voice came over the loudspeaker, speaking English in a precise sing-song. "The sheriff has decided to take a nap." It was Chiun.

"Sorry, girls," Remo said.

They attacked him. Nails, fingers, feet and breasts clawed and hammered at him. They all missed. Then Remo had the girls from behind, an arm around each, holding them by the boobs and he dragged them past the water-lasers, to the gash in the earth that was the San Andreas fault.

He tossed them in. They hit with a thud, eight feet below him, and lay there, stunned. Remo turned back to the two water-lasers. They were screaming now, building up pressure, ready in moments to start pouring their gallons of water down into the shaft, a concentrated spurt of force that could tear a state apart.

Remo looked for switches. The machines still thumped. He couldn't find out how to turn them off.

He put his hands on the coupling which joined the machines to the shaft and wrenched. The coupling snapped loose and just at that instant, the water started to pour out of the end of the tubes.

The jarring force of the pressure paralyzed Remo's arms. He spun. The water poured out in a powerful cohesive stream. With all his strength, Remo aimed it down toward the ground, into the fault.

The water was barrelling now into the crack in the earth. Then the earth groaned, and as Remo watched in fascination, the earth began to close up. The girls screamed, then the sound stopped as the earth closed over them, then the lasers ran dry.

Remo looked down at where the gouge in the earth had been.

"That's the biz, sweethearts," he said.

Two lives against maybe a million. Still, they had had great tits.

The ground shook again and Remo was knocked off his feet. He fell heavily on his bleeding shoulder. Another grenade, he thought.

But it was no grenade. The ground rocked and vibrated.

A quake, Remo realized in horror. But how? The water-lasers had been disconnected.

He labored his way to his feet, unsteady on the

ground. He took a step in one direction. No, the force was coming from the other direction.

Had they set another device, timed to go off? Why then had they been working on this one?

Remo took off, over the shaking ground, racing along the rocky ledge, trying to find the source of the power. He ran heavily and he realized he was losing blood from the shrapnel wound. Then a tiny figure in black flashed by him, passing Remo as if he were standing still, out-distancing him, racing far ahead. It was Chiun, the Master of Sinanju, running across the shifting, sliding earth as if it were a cinder track.

Remo ran full sprint but Chiun pulled ahead. While Remo's legs pumped, pushing him forward against the shifting thrusting ground, Chiun seemed to glide motionless, moving through an inner momentum, the legs just keeping pace. Chiun pulled farther ahead into darkness.

Birds called, shrill caws of danger from their aerial safety. Remo saw a fear-crazed collie run at him and stumble into a somersault, its hind legs pumping furiously as though running uphill. The earth churned and the air was thin.

Into the brush Remo ran, cutting himself on brambles that came lurching at his face. Then he was in a clearing, and there, rising on long aluminum stilts like the shell of an unfinished steeple, was a giant water laser, twenty times larger than the ones Remo had seen before. And in this clearing, a half-football field wide, was stillness, a stillness surrounded by earth amok. It was as though a still hand suspended from an aloof moon held it placid in a sea of chaos. The earth smelled of ozone, the calls of the birds were muffled as though the vibrations of their sounds sucked from the air.

Beneath the stilts knelt Dr. Quake. But he was not

in prayer. He was in pain, and this Remo knew because the black robed figure of Chiun stood over Dr. Quake, one hand on the neck as if squeezing a collared pigeon.

Remo almost fell because of the sudden quiet of the earth. His reflexes were attuned to the previous vibrations and still reacting to them. This upset was only momentary; he moved to the pair quickly.

Remo heard Dr. Quake groan:

"It can't be stopped. No one can stop it. It feeds on its own progression. It generates itself."

"That which is started can be stopped." Chiun's voice was even and as distant as the moon.

"They wouldn't listen to me. If they had listened I wouldn't have done this," said Dr. Quake.

Chiun released the hold on the neck.

"He has told all he knows," Chiun said.

"Where are Jacki and Jill, my daughters?" sobbed Dr. Quake looking at Remo. "They were supposed to meet me here."

"They're where they belong," said Remo. "How do you stop this machine?"

"It can't be stopped," sobbed Dr. Quake.

"He tells the truth," said Chiun. "He surrendered to the pain and has told all he knows." Chiun looked up the aluminum stilts of the water laser. "Is this the machine with no vibrations?"

"Yes," said Dr. Quake.

"It's going to blast water into the lock at tremendous pressure," Remo said to Chiun. "The state is going to snap along the fault." He had to yell just so his voice sounded normal.

"Is this space here free of vibrations because the machine has harnessed them?" asked Chiun.

"Yes," said Dr. Quake.

"You are wrong,' said Chiun. "Everything that moves has vibrations. Life is vibrations."

"That's your philosophy, not science," said Dr. Quake. Then he cried for his daughters and called them his poor innocent babies.

Chiun looked at Remo.

"If this is your science and this is what it has brought you, then I say your science is false. Life is vibration, movement is vibration, being is vibration. The universe is a vibration. Your science has created a machine that appears to have forgotten vibrations. I will have to remind it."

"Chiun?" said Remo. He wanted to warn but knew not how

"You believe that science is one thing and the spirits of man another."

"Chiun, this is a machine. If it were a thousand men, little father, I would not doubt you."

"It is all one," said Chiun, and he briefly surveyed the long stilts and the giant metal nozzle pointing into the belly of the earth. "I will remind this insolent machine of its vibrations."

"We're all doomed," yelled Dr. Quake with laughter that was despair, a final not-caring before the end.

"Fool," said Chiun to the kneeling figure. And his black robe disappeared up the stilts. Remo could discern only an edge of the robe outlined against the moon at the pinnacle of the steeple.

The robe fluttered once and then the earth seemed to explode. The muffling silence became a shriek as if someone had clanged cymbals in Remo's ears. The stillness became a giant snap as if someone had pulled strings on Remo's legs; he was suddenly somersaulting, his legs flying wildly. Then a tremendous vibration slapped Remo's finely tuned body almost to the cracking point. He was on the ground.

184

Blood filled his mouth. He could not focus his eyes.

He was rolled over, and he saw the moon as a fuzzy yellow bulb above him. He groaned and then breathed. Something blocked the moon. He heard Chiun's voice. Chiun was standing over him.

"It broke. Heh. Heh. Nothing works in America except me."

"Ooh," said Remo. "What happened?"

"I taught this little device to remember its vibrations."

"Don't let Dr. Quake escape," said Remo. He felt wet coolness envelop his back.

"Escape? He was in even worse condition than you. He is dead, his body unable to accept a little buffeting."

"A little buffeting? I almost died."

"Last year you ate a hamburger with ketchup and said that would not harm you. Two years ago it was a steak. And even at your Christmas time you consumed a bubbling drink laden with sugar, yet now you complain of a little buffeting."

"Will I make it?"

"Not if you kill your body with your mouth."

"I mean will I be able to walk again? Have I bought the package?"

"You mean will you return to your former standards of shoddy performances, gross eating habits and disrespect?"

"You like to take advantage of the helpless, don't you?"

"When I tell you to consume only healthy foods, I am helping you. But you do not wish to be helped. When I tell you proper mental attitudes, you forget them and do not wish to be helped. Now you ask for help. How do I know you will take it?"

"I'll take it. I'll take it already, you sonuvabitch."

"Disrespect, you learn well."

"Please."

"Breathe to fullness," Chiun commanded, as though Remo were back in the first days of training, when he heard the elderly Oriental explain that all force came first from breathing.

The breathing was painful and then Remo felt another shock and he was on his feet. Water puddled around his ankles. Dr. Quake's body was folded in two, his chin resting on his groin, his spinal column snapped. Behind him the aluminun spire had also snapped, and water gushed harmless undirected from two large pipes.

The moon played golden on the sloshy wet ground. The birds no longer called in hysterical shrieks. The California night air tasted fresh and good and rich.

"When the machine remembered its vibrations, it died," said Chiun.

"That explains it," said Remo. "How are you with electric toasters?"

"Better than you young white men," said Chiun, using what Remo knew was Chiun's ultimate insult.

"You wouldn't happen to know the geological result of all this, would you?" asked Remo.

"The earth is wounded and it will one day shriek in pain. I would not wish to be here when it yells."

"I guess that says it all."

# CHAPTER TWENTY-SEVEN

The mini-report over the telephone was a pleasure in its delivery. Smith was truly shocked that Dr. Quake had been behind the scheme. And suddenly Remo realized why.

"He was on our payroll. Admit it. One of ours. That's why you didn't think he was involved. Admit it."

"I don't know everyone who's on our payroll," Smith said dryly. Remo cradled the receiver in the crook of his neck. He had shut the door of the pay phone booth, apparently trapping a full third of California's insect population.

"Wow," Remo said. "That's something. You put a guy on the payroll who nearly destroys half of California."

"Don't forget the million and a half," Smith said.

"What a loser you turned out to be," Remo said.

But the click of the phone across the continent interrupted his gloating. The pleasure disappeared like the coin in the phone box.

Remo cracked open the box with a snap of his forefinger, shattering the lock. He opened the change vessel with a crush of his right hand and scooped up nickels, dimes and quarters. Then he threw them at the California moon. He missed.

**THE "BUTCHER,"**
the only man to leave
the Mafia—and live!
A man forever on the run,
unable to trust anyone,
condemned to a life
of constant violence!

THE BUTCHER SERIES

# Violence is a man! His name is Edge...

The bloodiest action-series ever published, with a hero who is the meanest, most vicious killer the West has ever seen.

## It's sharp — It's hard — It's EDGE

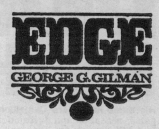

GEORGE G. GILMAN

PINNACLE
BOOKS

# THE INCREDIBLE, ACTION-PACKED SERIES

# DEATH MERCHANT

His name is Richard Camellion; he's a master of disguise, deception and destruction. He does what the CIA and FBI cannot do. They call him THE DEATH MERCHANT!

| Order | Title | Book No. | Price |
|---|---|---|---|
| _____ | #1 The Death Merchant | PO21N | 95c |
| _____ | #2 Operation Overkill | PO85N | 95c |
| _____ | #3 The Psychotron Plot | P117N | 95c |
| _____ | #4 Chinese Conspiracy | P168N | 95c |
| _____ | #5 Satan Strike | P182N | 95c |

and more to come ...